# WHEN EVERYTHING FEELS LIKE THE MOVIES
## *Governor General's Literary Award Winner*
(Children's Literature—Text)

"An edgy and uneasy story with no simple resolutions, Raziel Reid's *When Everything Feels like the Movies* is unflinching. An openly gay teen in a small-minded town, Jude Rothesay's fantasy life is a movie but his real life isn't. He is audacious, creative, rude, often hilarious and sometimes heartbreaking. He's unforgettable."
**—Governor General's Literary Award jury**

"His extravagant fantasies and irrepressible nature make Jude one of the most memorable teen characters in recent CanLit." **—CBC Radio**

"Even within the realm of YA books about gay, cross-dressing teenagers, *When Everything Feels like the Movies* stands out. It doesn't mince words, and often those words are the kind not generally found in children's literature."
**—*Montreal Gazette***

"A tightly constructed life-as-a-stage allegory, complete with filmic idolatry and requisite amounts of love, lust, and all associated melodrama." **—*Backlisted***

"A powerful first book, an important book for young queer youth, and written like a burst of glitter gushing through an open wound." **—*Lemon Hound***

# WHEN EVERYTHING FEELS LIKE THE MOVIES

## RAZIEL REID

Arsenal Pulp Press • Vancouver

US edition published 2015

FOURTH PRINTING: 2015

ARSENAL PULP PRESS
Suite 202–211 East Georgia St.
Vancouver, BC V6A 1Z6
Canada
*arsenalpulp.com*

The publisher gratefully acknowledges the support of the Canada Council for the Arts and the British Columbia Arts Council for its publishing program, and the Government of Canada (through the Canada Book Fund) and the Government of British Columbia (through the Book Publishing Tax Credit Program) for its publishing activities.

This is a work of fiction. Any resemblance of characters to persons either living or deceased is purely coincidental.

Cover photograph: Getty Images © Frank P. Wartenberg
Design by Gerilee McBride
Edited by Susan Safyan

Printed and bound in Canada

Library and Archives Canada Cataloguing in Publication:
Reid, Raziel, 1990–, author
    When everything feels like the movies / Raziel Reid.

Issued in print and electronic formats.
ISBN 978-1-55152-574-7 (pbk.).—ISBN 978-1-55152-575-4 (epub)

    I. Title.

PS8635.E433W46 2014      C813'.6      C2014-904529-8

                                    C2014-904530-1

*I guess I am a fantasy.*
—Marilyn Monroe

# *Preproduction*

I would've gone down for a pair of Louboutins (I think they call that "head over heels"), but the closest I ever got was kissing the feet of celebrities in tabloid magazines.

My mother's closet was basically a sex shop. It was full of costumes and shoes, which she wore to work. That's "work" in the original sense, although she werked for a living.

I'd take a pair of her shoes and wear them down in the basement, pretending the cement floor was covered with a red carpet and the washer and dryer were paparazzi. I hoped the conspiracy theory that the iPhone camera lens is the all-seeing eye was true. *Big Brother is watching you.* Perfect! I loved an audience.

Ray caught me once. It took me a while to notice him standing in the laundry room doorway because of all the white spots in my eyes. When I blinked, my world coruscated. He didn't say anything, just stared at me and then shook his head, turned off the light, and went back upstairs. I stood in the darkness, barely feeling my feet bleeding from the patent leather heels, which were too small and dug into my skin. I didn't care about the pain. My blisters were stigmata! I was their Jesus. I bled for them so that we could have life.

I remember what shoes I was wearing when we all got together for our first read-through, the summer before I had my brains blown out in heart-shaped chunks. I was flipping through a magazine, waiting for Angela at the graveyard gate in giant white platforms. They made me look like Baby Spice and Michael Alig's love child. I had a lollipop and a syringe filled with Drano tangled in the laces.

When Angela showed up, she said, "I brought my camera in case you want to shoot."

"You know you never have to ask to take my picture," I told her. "But if you ever do and I say no, keep taking it anyway. And don't stop until I have a mental breakdown."

"Tight boots," she said, lighting a joint.

"They're my mom's. She wears them when she dresses as a school girl and dances to 'Baby One More Time.' I totally helped choreograph her routine."

"Forty years old and still dressing like an underage slut," Angela laughed. "I think I'll make a Facebook fan page for her when I get home."

I licked a picture in the tabloid I was holding. "Sorry," I said, "I have to make the Hemsworth brothers as wet as they make me."

"No need to apologize, dude," Angela snapped a Polaroid. "I'd do them both at the same time."

"You'd do them both in the same hole," I laughed. "But who wouldn't?"

"Who do you think is bigger," she asked, "Chris or Liam?"

"Liam. He'd have to be to fill Miley."

We smoked while I climbed over tombstones, posing like a starlet corpse. My pale skin made me look like a wraith. I was one with the white flash. Angela took Polaroids because she thought they made her bohemian, which is the same reason why she smoked cigarettes and had unprotected sex.

I wasn't surprised when she got a text from one of her boyfriends and immediately got horny and said she had to go. Angela is a transient being. A hard, fast volt. She asked if I wanted to walk home with her, but I decided to stay. I loved the graveyard. It was filled with so many flowers—it was like the Elysian Fields. Whenever I was there, I'd imagine I was a god walking around in ten-inch hooker heels. Or, depending on my mood, just a hooker.

Angela gave me a joint before leaving, kissing both my cheeks goodbye. She planted her big wet lips right on my skin. It was like she wanted to leave a part of herself on me. She had to mark her territory and make sure she wasn't forgotten. I think that's why she wore so much perfume. Angela always reeked. Everyone told her she smelled like a whorehouse, but I think she took it as a compliment.

"You can keep the Polaroids," she called back as she started heading down the path. "I know how obsessed you are with yourself. Just don't get them all sticky this time!"

I lit the joint when she was gone, and while I smoked I gave an interview to a tombstone like it was Barbara Walters. I was always imagining I was on her "Most Fascinating People" list. Number one, obviously.

Barbara had just started to make me cry when I heard them come up behind me. I quickly wiped away my tears as Matt rolled down the path on his skateboard. But it was Luke I saw first, lagging behind him with his hands in his pockets. My irises shuttered like the lens of a camera.

Kenny and Colin followed, both looking like Aberzombies just burst from graves. I felt sorry for them. They needed so much plastic surgery.

"Judy!" Matt said, excited to see me. I was his favourite entertainment, the show he couldn't turn off (or on, for that matter). Matt thought he was so hot, but he was the same height as Justin Bieber. Even their egos were the same size. I jerked off thinking about him once, but only because Angela described his dick as "prodigious." He snatched the joint out of my manicured hand before I could stop him.

"I wouldn't smoke that," Colin told him. "You might get the hiv."

"Ew, that like doesn't even exist anymore," I said, rolling my eyes. "What decade are you from?"

Matt made a big show of wiping off my contamination anyway before bringing it to his mouth.

"Nice boots," he sneered. Smoke coiled out of his mouth—he was a snake. I started to walk off, and he skated after me. The others followed—I guess they wanted autographs too. Matt passed Luke the joint and he took a long puff, holding the smoke at the back of his throat until his eyes burned. "I said I like your boots," Matt said, picking up his board and blocking my way. He shoved my chest. "You don't thank someone when they compliment you?"

"Ugh," I sighed, like he was an overzealous fan. "Fuck off, you stalker."

"That's not very nice," Matt smirked, getting in my face. He totally wanted to kiss me. "I've seen them before, you know. Your mom was wearing them when I tucked a dollar bill between her tits."

I pushed him, harder than I thought I could without breaking a nail. He seemed surprised when I knocked him to the ground, but quickly recovered and jumped back up. "I've always wondered what it would feel like to punch a girl," he said, swinging at me. I flinched, protecting my face, and he missed, but I lost my balance in the platforms and fell onto a grave.

"Let's just get out of here," Luke sighed, acting bored so that I wouldn't end up *in* the grave. Yet. He passed Matt back the joint to distract him. Matt took it, blowing smoke in my face.

"I know you're used to being on your knees, Judy," Matt said, "but for the last time: no, you cannot suck my dick."

I jumped up and spat in his face as if it had been choreographed. I did my own stunts!

"Dude," Kenny said to Matt, disgusted. "You're totally going to get pink eye!"

"Yeah," Colin laughed, "pink triangle eye."

I almost laughed too, not just because Colin had said something witty for the first time in his life, but because I was nervous. I didn't usually fight back, aside from blowing kisses, and something told me I was about to pay for it.

Matt's skateboard came for my head before I could duck. He kept hitting me even when I was down. Later, the doctors worried that he'd injured the ventromedial prefrontal cortex part of my brain, which can leave you without morals or compassion. I was disappointed that it wasn't damaged, because wouldn't it be nice not to give a shit? Blood streaked down my face like I'd been punctured by my crown of thorns as I lay upon a spike of asphodels. At least that's how I chose to remember it. Cinematography is so crucial.

When I came to, the park was empty, and the blood was pooling in my nostrils. I told myself it was a performance, and I was up for an award—I was up for all of them. I tried to stand to make my acceptance speech but got dizzy and fell back down. When I opened my eyes again, I thought I had died and gone to heaven because Luke was looking down at me.

"Shit," is all he said as he gave me his hand and helped me up. I couldn't believe I was touching him. The shock gave my heart back its beat. He let me lean on him as we walked out of the graveyard onto the abandoned street. I got blood all over his shirt. The hospital was only a couple blocks away, but I was staggering. I acted like I couldn't hold my head up just so that I could lean on his shoulder.

He lit us a joint. It was like he didn't know what else to do. He tried to get me to take a puff, as if I'd be okay if I could at least take a puff. He basically shoved it in my mouth. *Fantasy fulfilled.* The joint fell to the sidewalk, and I wasn't sure if the red smudges were from my lipstick or my blood.

I told him I loved him. I just said it like it was written in the script. I always thought I'd say it with a tear, but it didn't come. The director could only expect so much from me when I was under pressure. I felt Luke freeze up, like he was about to push me away, like he was going to let me fall to the sidewalk and crawl the rest of the way to the hospital while he ran in the other direction in his bloody shirt, pretending he bought it with the red splatters at some store in the mall where they spray cologne until you're choking and play music so loud you feel like you should be doing a bump every time you go to the change room. But he didn't push me away. Luke had no imagination. He helped me the rest of the way to the hospital and left me on the stairs next to a nurse who was on her smoke break. I thought the step was still his pec until I shivered from the cold.

I hoped he might come to the hospital to visit me while I was recovering. I sat in my bed waiting, and when he didn't show up, I was so furious that I almost told the tabloids, I mean the police officer, everything when she asked about the boy who dropped me off. "Did he do this to you?" she asked. But I kept my mouth shut, even about Matt, because I knew that Luke would go down with him. And maybe that's what he deserved, but I wouldn't do it. I wouldn't destroy the only memory of him that showed he felt something too.

Once the stitches had healed, Angela would touch the scar on my forehead and say, "You're a wizard, 'arry," every time she was stoned.

I saw Luke again on the first day of school. I was in the bathroom touching up my face when he walked in. The tap stopped running, and the only sound was the water swishing through the drain in the wall like hushed gossip. He came over to the sink next to me and put down his backpack. Our eyes met in the mirror before he turned to look at me. At the real me. I was sure that the reflection in the mirror was just another scene from the movie always playing in my mind; I was scared that if I looked away and faced him, the screen would fade to black. So I stood perfectly still as the reflection of his hand came toward my face like the most beautiful special effect ever created. He traced my scar slowly, from top to bottom, then looked down at the makeup on his fingertip and smiled.

## *Hair and Makeup*

It was the beginning of the end. The first day back to school after winter break. I had to hit snooze, or I'd have had a breakdown by third period. When I finally woke up, my eyes squinted from the light shining through the snow packed against my basement bedroom window. The dog-piss streaks were glistening like the yellow brick road, blinding me. All I wanted for Christmas was a sleep mask, but my grandma said Santa thought I was already too dramatic.

Stoned Hairspray started licking my face. Her tongue felt like sandpaper, but it was my favourite feeling in the world. She was purring so hard my mattress vibrated. Stoned had brown- and caramel-coloured fur and yellow eyes. She followed me home one day, and I decided to keep her because Ray was allergic to cats. My mom said she couldn't stay, but I promised to keep her in the basement where Ray almost never went. There was nothing down there but my bedroom and the laundry room, both of which he avoided. So Stoned became my cellmate, making prison life more bearable. Angela and I named her Stoned Hairspray on account of huffing a can of hairspray when we were trying to come up with a name. It just sort of stuck.

When Stoned was done cleaning my face, I reached for my laptop on the floor so I could Facebook stalk Luke Morris. He still hadn't accepted my friend request. I jerked off to my favourite picture of him, which he'd posted from his family's cabin during the summer. He was standing on a dock, and his swim trunks were wet. If you looked closely, you could see the outline of his crotch. That did it every day. Usually more than once.

I had a new comment on one of my Facebook pictures, the one I took in Photo Booth where I'm posing like an underage girl doing a Terry Richardson shoot who actually thinks dreams come true. The comment was from Kenny Randal. He wrote, "faggot!!!!!" with five exclamation marks. I don't know why I bothered with my privacy settings when Facebook just went back to default every time a bored Zuckerberg got even more Orwellian.

I almost deleted the comment, but decided to keep it like another badge from the Pretty Boy Scouts.

When I went upstairs to shower, I saw my mom was in the kitchen, burning pancakes. She'd just gotten home from work and was still dressed like a slutty nurse. Keefer sat at the kitchen table playing a game on his DS. All I could hear were gun shots and screams. The shower steamed up the bathroom mirror, and when I got out, I drew a heart so I could see my reflection. The steam streaked it, and it looked like the heart was bleeding.

I used my mom's eyeliner and pink lip gloss, and then sprayed some of her Mademoiselle in my wet, dirty-blond hair. The bottle I'd stolen from her was already empty. My hair was almost down to my shoulders—long enough that I was always getting mistaken for a girl, which I liked. Tranny chasers are so hot.

I stared at my reflection in the perspiring glass, tucking my dick between my legs and pursing my sticky pink lips. I was transparent; I could've already been a ghost. Every mirror I looked into turned to water, and I was always ready for my close-up. Since I was born by caesarean, I wasn't deformed from childbirth. My mom said all the nurses and parents told her how beautiful I was. "Lord knows you were no immaculate conception," she laughed, "but you sure were immaculate."

In the first picture ever taken of me, I'm lying in the hospital nursery wrapped in a yellow blanket. Not blue like all the other baby boys or pink like all the girls. It was a yellow blanket, which I kept my whole life. I'd sleep with it every night. Even when I was too old and it embarrassed me, I loved it. But then I always loved things that didn't love me back.

I used to wonder if the parents who looked at me and my yellow blanket in the nursery with all the other babies thought I was a little boy or girl. If it mattered. If, on my first day on earth, I wasn't either.

I was just beautiful.


When I was done with hair and makeup, I was ready to start filming. I walked to school, but imagined I was in LA. I turned the bungalows with snow piled on decaying shingles into

Beverly Hills mansions. The dogs tied up in backyards, sticking their frozen noses in the air and barking, became the honking horns of limos with starlets overdosing in the back. The mine was a studio lot. The thick grey smog that hovered over town was the pollution from a traffic jam on the Hollywood Freeway. I zigzagged down the sidewalk, slipping on ice and pretending it was the Walk of Fame.

I'm not going to tell you what town I lived in because it was a dump, and it will just depress you. It had everything you needed if you didn't need anything at all. The movie theatre only had one screen, which played one movie a week, and it was usually a couple months old. We always got things a little later than everyone else, once they had trickled through the rest of the world. The town had one newspaper, which you could read cover to cover on the toilet and still have time to raid the medicine cabinet for anything that might help you catch a buzz. There was a mine where almost everyone worked, including my dad before he died.

The funeral scenes were tragic. It was always a gruesome death. Usually I killed him off in a car accident that left him decapitated like Jayne Mansfield. If I wanted real tears, I'd think of her. My father always came back from the dead like a Soap Star, so maybe that's why I cried for Jayne, because she couldn't. Her heart only beats on a screen in the dark.

When I stepped through the school doors, my fans went crazy. I had arrived just in time for the end of morning announcements. Our principal, Mr Callagher, was saying through the speaker that the school was throwing a Valentine's dance, and if anyone wanted to help organize it, they should come to the office at lunch and shove their finger up his ass.

Everyone was busy talking about what they got for Christmas and how wasted they got on New Years. No one gave a shit about Mr Callagher. His voice boomed overhead like God's, but no one was a believer. Hadn't he seen the portraits of him scribbled on the tables in the caf? Pants down, hairy balls, pencil dick up Janitor Jim's ass.

They made portraits of me, too. They were my graffiti tabloids. I was totally famous. I'd imagine that the drawing in the handicap stall of my alleged crotch with "Hermafrodite Jude/ Judy" scribbled next to it was the cover of the *National Enquirer.* Misspelled headline included. I was addicted to them. I'd look all over the bathroom and on all the walls in the hallway, and if there wasn't one waiting for me on my locker for Jim to paint over at the end of the day, I was crushed. I wanted them to hate me; hate was as close to love as I thought I'd ever be.

While Mr Callagher made his announcement, I stared at Luke, who had morning wood sticking out of his gym shorts. I couldn't believe it. It made the crotch-shot on the dock seem amateur. I don't think he even noticed; he was looking bored and tapping his foot on the floor. He was wearing the shoes with Madison's lip print still smudged on the side. The shoes were his Christmas present. Of course, she had to give them to him on the last day of school, five days before Christmas, in front of everyone. Standing right in the middle of the hall, she took one of the white Nikes out of the box and kissed it. She wore a glossy red lipstick that made her lips look juicy, like she had just sucked on a tampon, which I'm pretty sure she did once just to get her YouTube channel more views. Luke seemed embarrassed as Madison passed him the lipsticked shoe. He was smiling, but it was like he was being forced to take a picture first thing in the morning before he'd even had a chance to rub one out or eat a Pop-Tart.

Mr Callagher was reminding everyone that smoking was forbidden on school property as Luke crossed his hands on his lap to hide his bulge—or rub against it. Probably both. He stared straight ahead and barely blinked. His thick eyelashes were so dark that it looked like he bought them at the drugstore, like I do. I fantasized about gluing them on his eyes and then ripping them off as he climaxed. I wondered what he was thinking about. I wanted to crawl into his head and see what I needed to be to become the thing that he was thinking about.

When Mr Callagher was done speaking, Brent Mackenzie asked Mrs Kennedy if she'd go to the Valentine's dance with him, which made a few people laugh. The few who'd been lucky enough to wake 'n' bake. Mrs Kennedy did her best to look unimpressed, but her cheeks were as red as a spanked ass in a BDSM porno. I would know. Angela and I watched all the DVDs in the box under her parents' bed, like, twice.

## The Set

My middle school was basically a movie set. No one was real. Especially me. We were all just playing our parts. You might be sort of real when you start school but you're quickly typecast and learn all your lines by rote—mostly because you've written them in detention so many times.

Everyone fell into one of three categories:

1. The Crew: They made things happen. They took over the honour roll, sports teams, extracurricular activities, and clubs. They had the most volunteer credits and were first to raise their hands whenever the teacher asked a question. They weren't necessarily the smartest, most talented, or prettiest, but they were involved. Without the crew, nothing would ever get done, and we'd all be wandering down the hallways in search of our marks.

2. The Extras: All the misfits, outcasts, and social rejects. If you were as chipped as my nail polish and didn't belong, you were an extra—kind of the opposite of the Crew. They were there, but you didn't really know it; they were just bodies in

desks filling space, anonymous smiles in faded school photos on a boulevard of broken dreams.

3. The Movie Stars: No one thinks they're more special than they do, but everyone wants to be tagged in a Facebook picture with the stars and get their autographs in the yearbook. They're selfish, spoiled, and overly sexed. There isn't much beyond the surface of their flawlessly airbrushed skin, and everyone talks about them behind their backs. Their eyes light up when you can do something for them, and everything that comes out of their mouths is totally fake.

I didn't fit into any category. I definitely wasn't a part of the Crew; I wasn't about to be involved in anything unless it was court-appointed. I wasn't an Extra because the last thing I could ever be was anonymous. But I wasn't a Movie Star either because, even though everyone knew my name, I wasn't invited to the cool parties.

So there was me, the flamer that lit the set on fire.

I was usually in the spotlight, but every now and then I felt like Norma Desmond because the spotlight would fade, and I would be forgotten. That's when I would wear the most makeup, or throw myself to the floor in the middle of the hallway, like I had just tumbled out of a limousine after snorting an eight ball.

When I was in the spotlight, they all stared. Matt asked, "New lipstick, Judy?" Even though it was the same one I always wore, which he already knew, because he was so desperate for me to leave a ring of it around his prodigious cock.

The studio renamed me Judy the day Matt added a "y" to my name on the attendance list. Mrs Kennedy said "Judy" during roll call, and everyone burst out laughing. Poor Mrs Kennedy. She was so clueless. She kept calling "Judy Rothesay?" and asking if we had a transfer student.

It became my official stage name when the media picked up on it. Every time I walked down a hall/red carpet, the reporters would call me "Judy" to try to get my attention, but I'd refuse to comment. I'd turn their dirty looks into camera flashes and make them my paparazzi. They'd scream my name, and I'd let them take a little piece of my soul with each flash. Why not? They were going to take it anyway. The flashes would dim, and then the fluorescent hallway lights would again illuminate pimples and the dark circles you get from all-nighters spent either reading a text book or doing lines off of one. Everything would become real again.

Even the teachers watched me, like they wanted to remember every detail so that one day they could tell *People* magazine "I knew him when" for a pay-out bigger than their measly salaries. I had a faculty fan club that wrote me love letters. I saw one on Mr Dawson's desk. I was having lunch in his classroom, like I sometimes did when I felt like making him my Paula Strasberg. I'd refuse to step on set without him.

I liked Mr Dawson. He looked like an Old Hollywood movie star with finger waves and eyes that would still be beautiful in black and white. I had this weird thing for him. I wanted him to be my father, and I wanted to blow him.

Story of my life.

I saw the letter when he went to the teacher's lounge to get another cup of coffee. I didn't go looking for it or anything—it was just there. I got up to check out the books on the shelf behind his desk and my name jumped off the page. It was signed by Mr Callagher:

*We have a student who has decided to express his sexuality by sometimes wearing makeup or girls' clothing. As long as he isn't breaking the dress code, this is permitted. Some students don't seem bothered, while others have been more sensitive to the issue. We ask that you communicate with your class: they don't have to like it, but they have to respect the student's rights. Keep an eye on the situation for any problems, and please contact me with questions or concerns.*

I was tempted to steal the letter and have it framed, but I wasn't quick enough. Mr Dawson walked back into the room complaining about how weak the school's coffee was. I just kept thinking: they don't have to like "it."

"It" was another one of my stage names. It was my JLo. People meant to be insulting, but I found It empowering. I always thought they were referring to the Stephen King novel because of my ability to shape-shift into their greatest fear. It's amazing what a pair of heels can do.

When Angela still hadn't shown up by English, I was worried that she had passed out in a ditch again. I checked my phone under my desk, but there were no messages. I went on Twitter and saw that @mmcmillan was trying to trend #WhyJudyShouldDie. Matt Macmillan. He was my number-one fan. @Madisonsmusings retweeted and wrote, "bcuz no one would miss him." Madison Sinclair, a girl about as sweet as the blood that gushed out of the cuts in my arm every time I thought about her. @KennyRan tweeted, "so we can PARTY!!!!!" with five exclamation marks again. One for each of his brain cells.

"Mr Macmillan, eyes up please," Mr Dawson said to Matt. "Don't you think I know when you're on your phone? Seriously, no one just looks down at their crotch and smiles."

"Yeah?" Matt laughed. "You seen my crotch, Mr D?"

After English was gym, which was my favourite class because I got to see all the boys in their underwear. Plus, Mr Mead didn't care if I participated; he actually seemed relieved when I didn't, because if I didn't have to change, he didn't have to figure out which change room I should use. Not that his indecision stopped me from sneaking down to the boys' room for my daily peep show.

I was sitting on the sidelines when Angela showed up. As soon as I saw her, I remembered about her doctor's appointment. She told Mr Mead that she had cramps and came to sit next to me. She never changed into gym clothes either, but she wasn't going to fail gym. Mr Mead knew how to deal with her heavy flow as well as with my painted nails.

"How'd it go this time?" I asked her.

"I asked the doctor if he could suck out some fat when he took the fetus, and the nurse looked at me like I was masturbating with a crucifix."

"Why are crucifixes sexy?" I asked. "Because there's a naked man on them!" A whistle blew, and everyone started running laps. "Mr Mead is such a sadist," I said, admiring Luke as he ran past.

"Look at that tongue action," Angela said. "It's a whistle, not a clit!"

"You know you want me!" I yelled after Luke. He didn't even flinch, but Madison flipped me off and called me a faggot.

"Go get date raped, bitch," Angela yelled, and Mr Mead pretended not to hear. Madison just kept running, her bleach-out bouncing off her shoulders.

"Anyway," Angela sighed, taking off her jacket. "Do I look skinnier?"

At lunch, we went to the Day-n-Nite and sat in our usual back booth. I didn't bother opening the menu; I had it memorized. We always came to the Day-n-Nite, mostly to get away from everyone else who went to McDonald's.

We'd made the back booth ours ever since Angela slept with her second cousin and started keeping a list under the table. We always sat there because she always had a new name to add.

"Alexis tweeted, 'bcuz satan's hungry,'" I told Angela, passing her my phone to show her the #WhyJudyShouldDie thread.

"Alexis is the one who's hungry," she said, rolling her eyes. "You should tweet about her bulimia. Have you smelled her breath lately?"

"I sit behind her in Spanish."

"They can't get over you, can they?" Angela asked, like she was jealous. I swear, she was only happy if there was something nasty written about her behind a hashtag. Sometimes I thought she had shaved her head just so people would call her a dyke. When someone wrote "muffin muncher" on her locker, she just laughed and drew a muffin with a big smile and razor-sharp teeth. She claimed she shaved her head because she was a Buddhist, but the shave lasted only until her hair grew into a pixie-cut. I shaved my head once too, but just because I wanted to be like Britney Spears.

"Luke wrote something," I said, looking down at my phone.

"Since when can that retard type?"

"He wrote, 'so that the school doesn't have to make him his own bathroom.'"

"Madison is deluding herself with him. Did I tell you he passed me a note asking if I can deep throat?"

"He really is a retard if he had to ask," I said, maybe a little edgier than I intended.

"Don't worry, dude," she laughed. "I would never do that to you."

Brooke, the Day-n-Nite's waitress who hated us because we never tipped, but loved us because we didn't squeeze her ass when she walked past like all the truckers at the bar, took our order. After she walked away, I turned to Angela and asked, "I wonder if anyone's ever seen your list?"

"Probably some kids," she shrugged. "Who else goes under tables?"

"You and number four," I said. "And number twelve, if I remember correctly."

When I got home from school at the end of the day, the house was empty.

I danced down the hall into my mom's room. It smelled like perfume and sweaty sheets. I could see the imprint of Ray's body in the lumpy mattress. I went straight for the closet. It was all my mom's things; Ray used only two drawers in the dresser. The top and bottom of the closet were piled with shoes. There were so many that I kind of lost my breath every time I saw them. I took out the black dress that I tried on before because I knew it fit, and I wasn't sure how much time I had. It was short, lacy, and you didn't need boobs to fill it out. I got the dress on fast and picked through my mom's hairpieces but decided not to put them on because it took too long to take them out, and I wasn't sure how much time I had. Plus, her hair was dark, and I only wanted to be blond. Blonds have *more*.

I put on some jewellery instead, a couple of bracelets and a cubic zirconia ring with a rusted band. I tried on a few pairs of shoes, but my heart was already set on the thigh-high boots that made me look like Julia Roberts in *Pretty Woman*. Like I don't kiss on the mouth.

Once I was all dressed, I lit a cigarette out of a pack on the nightstand and sat on the edge of the bed, crossing my legs as I posed in front of the mirror.

Smoke coiled above my head like a halo.

## Child Star

My mother went off the deep end again. She was always going off the deep end. It was so annoying. Going crazy is never as glamorous as it looks on an *E! True Hollywood Story*.

Ray had disappeared. I didn't know where he went, and I don't think I wanted to, judging by how he looked when he eventually came home. I was just relieved that he had the decency to get lost every now and then. He was like an obnoxious commercial on TV that was louder than everything else and made you feel like you had just inhaled one too many whip-its.

I always knew when he was about to disappear because of all the little things: he'd tap his spoon against his bowl of cereal, stick his finger through the buttonholes in his shirt, and bite his lip like he was trying to chew it off. He'd be in the bathroom slicking back his black hair, and if there was one piece that had a mind of its own, he'd lose it. He'd go into a rage and break the comb or the mirror or anything stupid enough to get close to him.

"He's hot, but I bet he has raisin nuts," Angela said the first time she met him.

"He doesn't have 'roid rage," I told her. "He's just a maniac."

He did look like he was on steroids. He liked to show off his muscles and always wore wife-beaters. That was basically the extent of male fashion in my hometown. I'm surprised I lasted as long as I did.

Ray always pulled himself together for a few weeks, and then he'd fall apart again. He'd take the car, saying he was going to pick up some McDick's. Keefer would jump up and down screaming about the toy he wanted in his Happy Meal. My mom would tell Ray to bring her a strawberry milkshake, but I could tell by the sound of her voice that she knew he wasn't coming back.

When Ray was gone, my mom walked around with mascara-smudged eyes, drinking booze out of a coffee mug. Sometimes she'd even blow on it. She'd text him, but he'd never answer. Most of the time, he couldn't reply even if he wanted to because he had already sold his phone. She'd paint her nails and then nervously chip off the polish. She'd chain smoke and watch chick flicks because they gave her an excuse to cry.

This time, my mom was extra-hysterical that Ray was M.I.A. because we were having dinner with "Satan in a Sunday hat."

When we got to my grandma's house and she saw that Ray wasn't with us, she didn't seem surprised. She probably just thought he'd been in another meth lab explosion.

I knew it was really bad when my mom got wasted at dinner. She had stopped drinking in front of my grandma after my grandma wrote to A&E, trying to get our family on an episode of *Intervention*. But that night, my mom drank almost an entire bottle of gin at dinner, plus the bottle she drank before we drove over, so she was pretty drunk.

When my grandma told her to go freshen up in the bathroom, Mom picked her head up off her plate and stumbled off. We could hear her puking all the way down the hall. Keefer laughed, and my grandma just turned to me and asked, "More potatoes?" My grandma may have played pretend for all the wrong reasons, but I always admired how dedicated she was to her craft.

That night back at home, I had a dream about Luke. But this dream wasn't like all the others. He wasn't inside me. We were at the dance and everything in the gym was pink, like the walls had been painted with my nail polish. There was a big streamer over the stage that said "Happy Valentine's Day" and, even before I tasted it, I could tell by the way everyone was dancing that the punch had been spiked. I was wearing Glinda's pink ball gown, the one I'd stolen from the wardrobe department of my school's production of *The Wizard of Oz*. I took it as revenge when I didn't get cast as Glinda. Sometimes, I wore the dress alone in my room. It matched the walls in my dream, and I slid across the gym floor in graceful sweeps. Everyone turned and stared like they wanted a piece of me. But even in my sleep, I felt the timer in my heart. I knew that when the clock struck twelve, I'd wake up, and it would all be over.

Luke was standing in the middle of the gym wearing a tuxedo. He looked like a prince. And as I walked toward him in my gown like a lamb to the slaughter, I was his princess.

I woke up wet and jerked off thinking about him, but I couldn't come. The Luke fantasies were so overplayed in my mind that the images would sometimes lose their lustre, and I would have to think of some celebrity, or my dad, if I wanted to get off. Oh God, that reminds me … This one time, my grandma took me to see a shrink after I attempted suicide because I hated myself so much for jerking off to Chris Brown's nude selfie. Don't act like you haven't been there! I agreed to go only because I thought I'd get some free drugs out of it, but unfortunately he was the last doctor slow to reach for his prescription pad.

He kept asking me about my father because, before I had my first session, my mom called to tell the doc that it was all my father's fault. I only opened up to the shrink because he had signed a confidentiality agreement upon getting a guest role.

I don't have a lot of memories of my dad, but my earliest are of the feel of his stubble, the car grease stains on his blue jeans, and the way he always smelled of beer and cigarettes. There's a picture of us sleeping in bed together when I'm a baby, and I'm cradled in his arms with a pacifier in my mouth. He looks like a baby, too.

My mom was always yelling at him. She wanted more for him—she wanted more for herself. She totally became a stripper because she thought she was the next Anna Nicole Smith (RIP, you delicate angel) and was going to snag her very own J. Howard Marshall. But she just wasn't a gerontophile and became easily distracted by low-rent Romeos like Ray.

My dad didn't have any ambition. He thought he had it all so long as he had a six-pack of beer and his name tattooed on my mother's ass. But tattoos can be removed or covered over.

Maybe he was only comfortable with himself when he was on something that made him feel like he was someone else. In any case, he started ditching work at the mine to get drunk most days. After he got fired, my mom started working at the strip club. She used to tell me how he'd get into drunken rages, show up at the club, pull her off the pole, and try to beat up anyone who so much as looked at her. And the way she told me, it was like she was proud of him. She measured the depth of love by the deepness of the bruises.

I was about five years old when he got blackout drunk one night and refused to let her leave the house to go to work. I watched the whole fight from the hallway. He tied her up to a chair with a rope! It was so Sean Penn and Madonna, I had my first erection. Once she was tied up, I could tell my mom wasn't really afraid, but she still screamed at him. He just sat on the couch drinking his beer, taunting her and laughing to himself. A case later, he went from laughing to crying, professing his undying love, and promising to get his shit together.

Eventually, he passed out, leaving her tied up. When I heard my mom call my name, I crept into the living room to untie her. She didn't say anything, just looked at me through her smudged eyeliner and told me to go back to bed. I didn't tell her that I had pissed in it.

The weird thing was, things seemed to be okay between them for a few weeks after that. He sobered up, at least somewhat, and got the odd construction job. But when that didn't last, my mom decided to invest in our future by getting her first pair of implants. Nothing was ever the same.

My obsession with mirrors started the night she left him. I blame everything on my daddy issues, including my vanity.

Mom told me we were going to move into the convent, a.k.a. Grandma's house, until we got our own place. I thought that was the best idea in the world. Grandma had a pool. I could pretend I was Natalie Wood! I'd let a young Robert Wagner drown me any day. My dad got home from the bar just as we were leaving and went completely ballistic. Mom hit him first—she usually did. I stood and watched; it was like they didn't even register that I was there. Fists and furniture were flying. My dad pulled a full-length mirror from the wall and threw it across the room at my mom. She ducked, and it hit the wall next to where I stood. A piece of shattered glass cut my arm. When my dad saw that I was hurt, the rage in his eyes burned out, and he didn't try to stop my mom from taking me and leaving. He just fell back on the couch and stared at the blank TV screen.

His truck was parked in the driveway for a week. My mom wanted to go back and get the rest of our stuff, but he wouldn't let us in, even when she banged on the doors and windows and threatened to phone the police. We'd go sometimes at night, but the lights were always off. He was inside, sitting in the dark. He wouldn't answer my mom's phone calls, either. Then, one day, he was gone. His truck wasn't in the driveway anymore. When we went into the house to pack our stuff, we found a pile of broken heels next to the empty beer cans on the living room floor. It was like he had sat on the couch and broken each of her shoes, one by one. I can forgive my father most things, but not that.

When my dad left, and I realized that he wasn't coming back,

I'd console myself by imagining how badly he'd feel if he never saw me again because I had died—tragically and sensationally, of course. I'd pretend that, instead of abandoning me, he'd sold me to Disney, who won in a bidding war with the Discovery Channel to give me my own show. I became the most famous kid on the planet, the love child of Macaulay Culkin and Shirley Temple. An older Macaulay—when he's scorched from too much exposure to the spotlight and is skin and bones from heroin and idolization—and a young Shirley, in her six-year-old prime.

The letters from my stalker started coming when I got cast in a movie as a Boy Scout. I was pederastic cotton candy. My manager tried to hide the letters, but I found them. They were the first thing I ever masturbated to. I was a child star—quite jaded. The letters became more and more graphic: I want to nail you to a cross and cut off your phallus, I want to bite off chunks of your face, chew on them until they're mush, and then use it as lube. Security was beefed up, and I resented it. I had never been so adored. By that time, I was getting $10 million a movie, and I thought everyone should want to chew on my face. My stalker was my Shakespeare; his love sonnets were going to immortalize me. I started doing subtle things on screen, just for him. I'd lick my lips or even nibble them, if I wanted to make him go really crazy. For wide shots, I'd stick out my butt and arch my back. A few times, I even looked into the camera lens like it was his eyes.

My number-one fan got me in the end, in my sleep. The funeral had to be closed casket. There was a blown-up photo of me on the altar, the one I used to sign for fans who would line up for days to meet me—you know the one, above your bed? My dad couldn't bring himself to look at it. I was so retouched, I looked like a doll.

Everyone wanted to break me.

# The Small Screen

I went over to Angela's house so she could read my tarot. I brought a couple of roaches, which I stole from the ashtray on the nightstand next to my mom and Ray's bed. We didn't have a pipe or papers, and Abel was too busy playing guitar to open his door and lend us his bong, so we looked on YouTube to see what we could make.

"We're out of apples," Angela said, closing the tab. "But we have a can of Coke."

We went into the kitchen and took turns chugging it.

"This is so ratchet it better be on my Wikipedia one day," I laughed.

Angela took the first hoot back in her room. She made me take a picture of the smoke streaming out of her mouth so she could post it on Instagram. We could still hear Abel playing through the walls.

"It sounds like he's right next to us. Can you hear him masturbating?" I asked, not even trying to pretend I wasn't hopeful.

"I wear ear plugs. Mostly because my mom and dad's room is above mine and the ceiling is as thin as the walls."

"How often?"

"Fridays."

"Every Friday?

"Friday at ten, after the news."

"Glamour!"

"Do you ever hear your mom and Ray?"

"I'm surprised you haven't."

"Speaking of Ray," Angela picked the Devil card from the deck.

"Ugh, please let the next one you pull be Death."

She finished reading my cards, and I was excited because they said I was going to be famous.

"But you don't have any talent," Angela said.

"I do so! I write a killer suicide letter." I got up from the bed and went over to her mirror to put on some lip gloss.

"Are you sure you're gay?" Angela asked as she watched me. The sad thing is that she wasn't even being sarcastic. Angela wanted me. But I think that's mostly because I didn't want her and, gay or not, Angela thought every guy should want her.

"Of course not, Ange," I said. "I like beer and bitches and… Chanel Mademoiselle."

"You couldn't even get it up for me?"

"As desirable as you are, who would be the girl in the relationship?"

"I'd let you be the girl," she said, grabbing her pack of cigarettes and opening the window. "I wouldn't mind."

"You'd have to buy a strap-on."

"I'll steal my mom's."

"Your dad is freaky!"

"You don't think my mom actually uses it on him, do you?" she asked, shuddering as she lit a cigarette.

"Well, he's a cop."

"So?"

"He spends a lot of time in prisons..."

"It just isn't fair," she sighed. "We'd be perfect together."

"I don't know, you might get bored with me. I'm not enough of an asshole."

"Yeah, you wouldn't screw me over enough."

"And I wouldn't give you an STD. Isn't that, like, a prerequisite?"

"You're wrong," she said, blowing smoke rings. "You *are* enough of an asshole." There was a knock on the door and she asked, "Who is it?"

"Me," Abel said, poking his head in.

"I almost tossed a cigarette for you, jerk."

"Mom's pissed. You got a letter from school."

"For what?"

"Ditching class, failing class, indecent exposure in class... It really could be anything with you, couldn't it?"

"Bite me."

"Or me," I said from the vanity.

He didn't answer and didn't even look at me, but his face turned red.

"Are you constipated or something?" Angela asked.

"I heard you playing your guitar, Abel," I said, walking in front of him so he'd have to look. "You're really good."

"Thanks," he nodded, eyes to the floor.

"Is Mom home?" Angela asked.

"Bingo."

"You think she has any pills in her room?"

"I hear you're selling them now," I said to Abel. "How does it feel to be worshipped?"

"Anything good?" Angela asked.

He shrugged. "Pills. Mostly Seconals."

"Seconals?" I laughed. "Neely O'Hara lives!"

"Yeah, my mom's shrink is old school," Angela said. "He hands out the shit the FDA banned in the seventies."

"Your mother is so glamorous. She's like Sharon Tate, pre-stab wounds."

"She only has a couple pills left," Abel said.

"Or Marilyn pre-Kennedys."

"Don't take more than two," he insisted.

"Those fuckers ruined her," I told Angela, who just shook her head.

"She is not that glamorous."

"I took three and I couldn't move my legs," Abel said. "I couldn't feel anything."

"She dyes her hair from a box," Angela said.

"Did you know John Kennedy was bad in bed?" I asked her.

"I got so cold," Abel shivered.

"But I'm sure JFK Jr wasn't. I mean, you don't think?"

"And it looks yellow most of the time," Angela rolled her eyes.

"I would be so devastated."

"I was a fucking Vulcan," Abel said.

I made the Vulcan salute as Angela tossed her cigarette out the window.

"I'm going to check out the pharmacy," she said, brushing past her brother.

"I'm serious," he yelled after her, "don't take too many. She's going to notice."

As soon as she turned the hall corner, I closed the door and backed Abel against it. "If your mother doesn't notice the lipstick smudged on your dad's uniform," I said, almost touching his mouth with my lips, "then I highly doubt she'll miss a few dolls."

He didn't say anything, he barely even breathed. I wanted to kiss him, but I had to laugh. He was a sophomore, and all he really cared about was his guitar. He took a bong hoot every half-hour. I think he might've been in love with me, but I didn't love him back. I didn't even love Luke. I just wanted him to love me. I guess I wanted everyone to love me, but I don't think I loved anyone, really, except Keef. But that was different.

"Carly's coming over later," he said quietly because our faces were almost touching.

"Do you play your guitar and sing songs for her?" I asked.

"What?"

I kissed him.

"I'm serious," he said, pushing me away.

"But I like it rough," I said, and it sounded so sad coming out of my mouth that I wished I were deaf. I walked over to Angela's dresser and plucked a tissue from the box. "I smudged gloss on your lips," I said, slowly wiping it off. His lips parted as I touched them. I didn't know if it was because he was so nervous or because he wanted me to kiss him again. But when I tried to kiss him he held me back by my arms.

"Carly will taste you," he said.

I wondered what I tasted like.

He pushed me away when we heard Angela call from the living room. Abel opened the door and we walked down the hallway together, our arms touching until we reached the end and he stepped away from me. Angela was standing by the liquor cabinet, pouring vodka into two glasses.

"Find anything?" I asked as she passed me a drink.

"Some white things," she shrugged, dropping a couple in my hand.

"Exotic."

"You have to swallow them with booze because they don't work otherwise."

"Yes they do, you fiend," Abel said. He walked over and snatched one of the pills from her hand, popping it in his mouth like a Tic Tac.

"Well," Angela sighed, taking a gulp, "not as well."

Abel fell back on the couch while Angela took the bottle of Grey Goose to the kitchen and held it under the tap.

"How many times have we refilled that bottle?" I asked when she came back. "We're probably just drinking water."

I sat next to Abel on the couch as he turned on the TV, so close the hair on our arms got staticky and intertwined. I could tell he was holding his breath. Angela turned off the lights and did a few spins around the living room, her drink falling through the air like raindrops. We started to feel like our hearts were beating through the small screen. I watched a bead of sweat drip down the back of Abel's neck in the flickering light. He leaned forward, flipping through channels. The screen blurred, the pictures were kaleidoscopic, and it was like the channels were changing on their own. They flicked rapidly, like eyelids during an OD. The images changed so fast that all I could see were colours, bombs, blood, babies on fire, and stardom. Angela and I couldn't stop laughing. We dropped to the floor and wrapped ourselves in each other's arms. I buried my face in her hair. It smelled like lullabies. Like a lie. Abel was a statue. His eyes were as wide as disco balls; they spun as he watched the screen. As we entered it.

I unravelled myself from Angela, crawling toward Abel. He was perfectly still, on his mark, in his light. He looked pretty and plastic, like a mannequin. I took the remote from between his fingers. His knuckles were white from clutching it so tightly. I threw the remote at the screen, at my own head, and it went static. It was like the static was prickling and humming in our veins.

When Angela wasn't looking, I kissed Abel, and he came back to life. But he didn't kiss me back, so it was like kissing a Madame Tussauds wax figure. It was so quiet that I could hear him start blinking again. Then Angela, rolling on the floor, put her hand to her forehead and said, "Sometimes, when I close my eyes, it feels like I'm dying." I looked down at her. Even though everything was dark, the street lights outside were shining through the window, and I could make out her heart-shaped face. Sweat gleamed on her forehead as she rubbed her palms across the carpet. She closed her eyes and stopped moving.

"Is she dead?" Abel laughed, and everything felt so unreal.

I danced by myself while Abel rolled Angela onto her side so she wouldn't choke on her own vomit. I took his hand and led him to the couch. His skin was sticky, but I thought that was sweet. He fell back into the cushions like he was falling through clouds. He looked over my shoulder to make sure Angela was still extinguished and then climbed his hands up the curve of my spine. I licked a tear rolling down his cheek.

He wasn't blinking, like he was scared that if he did, we'd all drown.

## *Rehab*

When I woke up, my head was so heavy that I thought it was going to roll off my bed and crack on the floor. I never knew where the pills in Mrs Adams' pharmacy would take me, but it was always a journey, and a long way back.

Stoned Hairspray was on the other side of my door, meowing incessantly because she wanted in. Faded light shone through my window, which had snow packed against it.

I don't remember leaving Angela's. It must've been snowing when I walked home because my hair was still wet and knotted. I had already missed first period at school, and I took it as a sign that I shouldn't even bother with the rest of the day.

I let Stoned into my room and listened for any signs of life upstairs. The house was quiet. My mom was sleeping, Ray (he'd come back) was already at work for the day, and Keefer was at school. I climbed back into bed, kicking away my dusty sheets.

I hated the basement. I used to share a room with Keef until Ray decided it wasn't a good idea anymore. He wanted to protect his precious offspring from my glitter corruption. Ray brought down a rug and a dresser, and my grandma made me curtains, which I think were from one of her old tablecloths. Under my window, I hung up a picture of Marilyn Monroe, which I found in a dumpster, to cover the cracks, but the grey walls just made her eyes seem even more lost.

Then Angela and I went to the Sally Ann, and she distracted the clerk while I walked out with pillows and a lamp. The Salvation Army is run by a bunch of homophobic religious freaks, so we figured they had it coming. We took anything bright to make my new room seem like less of a prison. It didn't help; it still felt like there should be bars on the window.

I couldn't sleep the first night I spent in the basement. I tried to find the stars through my window—if the stars are spotlights, I wanted the sun—but the sky was empty. I started pretending the basement was a trendy rehab, because that gave me hope that I might one day get out.

I missed sharing a room with Keef. It was too quiet without him. He was a noisy sleeper who tossed and turned a lot and sometimes talked to himself. It was kind of nice, in a way. His mumblings were a welcome distraction when I lay awake at night, thinking the same things over and over—thinking of insane things and wishing it was over.

Keefer was the only one who didn't judge. Even when his friends at school teased him about me, he never brought it up. I wouldn't have known if he hadn't punched one of them once and gotten suspended. He wouldn't tell me what the kid said. Whatever it was, it was bad enough to make him lose his cool, which wasn't like him. He wasn't like his dad. I always thought he was sort of like me. Or what I would've been like if I had been like him, if that makes any sense. When I kept asking him what the kid said, he started crying. Keefer never cried. He was too busy pretending to be an action hero.

When I moved downstairs, it was weird for him too. Sometimes, if he had a bad dream or my mom was working or Ray was AWOL, he'd come down and sleep in my bed. I wouldn't have the heart to tell him to get lost.

One night, when I came home after sneaking out to meet Angela at the Day-n-Nite, he was there cuddled next to Stoned and drooling on my pillowcase. He woke up to the sound of my ripping shirt as I squeezed through the window.

"I didn't think you were coming back," he said, opening his crusty lashes.

This morning, my phone blew up with messages from Angela ranting about how she was in Bio and still feeling cross-faded from last night. I told her I was staying in bed for the rest of the morning, then went on Luke's page. If only Facebook stalking were illegal, my dream of being a prison bitch would have come true.

He'd posted two new pictures taken at a family meal during the holidays. The description on the first read, "Before," and it showed him with a huge plate of food—turkey, cranberry sauce, potatoes, gravy, veggies. In the next picture, "After," his plate was empty. His eyes were rolled to the back of his head, and he was smirking. I almost died because it was exactly what I imagined his come face would look like.

When I was done jerking off, I picked up one of the Old Hollywood star biographies, which I collected. They were scattered all over my room because a bookshelf was too big for me to steal from the Salvation Army. I was always reading about the old stars; if only they had taught Tinseltown Glamour at school, I probably wouldn't have needed Mrs Adams' personal pharmacy to help get me through the day.

I wanted to be them all. Well, all the girls. The only male star I ever wanted to be was James Dean. But that's just because he sucked so much dick.

I read for a bit and then tried to go back to sleep, but I wasn't really tired. I just lay there, twitching under the covers from thoughts that were like spider bites. I hugged Stoned Hairspray and closed my eyes, imagining she was Luke. Stoned had a way of wrapping her paws around my arm like she was holding it, like she knew what role she was playing. I imagined that Luke was holding me back. I could feel his breath on the back of my neck.

And it felt so real, I didn't know when I was dreaming.

When I woke up again, it was to the sound of creaking floorboards from my mom practicing her striptease.

I managed to crawl out of the window, shoving my way through the snow, and then I walked to the Day-n-Nite. I was supposed to meet Angela, but she texted to cancel because she was hooking up with some high school jock. "Just one?" I texted back, trying not to care that she was ditching me again. Everyone in Angela's life had a switch. She turned you on and then shut you off.

I was eating fries at the back booth by myself when the bells on the door rang. Luke and Madison walked in. I ducked so they wouldn't see me, watching as they slid into one of the black and pink leather booths. Luke put his arm around her, and I felt like I was going to throw up. I just wasn't sure if it was from grease or jealousy.

Although I was crouched down, Luke still saw me. Our eyes met for a second, and then he looked away and leaned forward to block me from Madison. He knew she'd make a scene. She was a Movie Star, after all.

I paid my bill with singles because my allowance always came from my mom's tips and then stood up and walked past them to make sure they saw me. Luke looked at the menu, and Madison called me a faggot. I loved the sound. Faggot is such a sexy word, it made me horny. That's what I wanted Zac Efron to call me when he finally took my virginity.

I didn't want to go home even though it was getting late. My mom would still be getting ready for work, and her stilettos would be cracking through the floorboards straight into my brain.

I never wanted to be home. It made me mental. But I never wanted to be anywhere, really. That was the problem; everywhere was the same. I was the same, no matter where I went. I put concealer on the dark circles under my eyes, but I was still a shadow.

I walked by the park to see if Abel was there, even though usually he was there only in the middle of the night; he was an insomniac. I started waking up to go sit with him. Looking up through the tree branches to the stars in the sky, I always felt an urgency to find the brightest one. Like if I found it first, it was mine.

The first time we met in the park, it was by chance. I walked past the entrance and saw his golden curls, the same colour as the dirty leaves stuck in the wet mud. I wouldn't have gone in if he hadn't been sitting on the graffitied park bench, staring out at the river. The park was creepy at night. The tree branches creaked like the devil on tiptoes, and the wind was like his breath over your shoulder. I liked Abel because he was easy to talk to and to not talk to. Sometimes we'd sit on the bench and not say a word, but it was okay.

I made it happen. Then, once it did, it was like there was no going back. It started near the beginning of the school year. I had gone to his house to see if Angela was home, but she was hanging out with one of her boyfriends. I'm not sure which one— number six on her list, I think. But it might've been number 666. Anyway, I was about to leave, but Abel called out to me halfway down the driveway and asked if I wanted to hang out. He put his hands in his pockets and shrugged from the door. His face was so red, I thought blood might spill out of his ears. I couldn't tell if "hang out" meant play Nintendo, roll on molly, or make out. But secretly, I hoped for all three.

We were home alone because Mr Adams was working and Mrs Adams was at the casino. We went to the living room, and he rolled us a joint while I flipped through daytime TV. I settled on *The Ellen DeGeneres Show* while he sparked it. "I am not a second-class citizen," Ellen said to the camera, tears in her eyes.

"Who died?" Abel asked, blowing a smoke ring that I popped with my accent nail. He passed me the joint, and after a few puffs, I already felt different. Like each time I batted my eyelashes, it was in slow motion. I looked at him through the smoke, lifting my hand to brush a curl out of his eyes. I took the lighter, which he'd dropped in his lap, and flicked the flame. He sucked on the joint so hard he must've got ashes at the back of his throat. His cough almost blew out the flame. He watched with watering, bloodshot eyes as I licked my finger and held it to the fire.

"It's a lovely way to burn," I told him, but he just stared at the commercials playing on the screen. I kept the flame burning and brought it closer to his face, so close it was like that time Angela tried to light the pipe for me and burned off some of my eyelashes. Abel didn't even flinch. I blew out the flame, and when my breath hit his face, his eyes closed. I waited for them to reopen, but they didn't. The roach burned out between his fingers as I placed the lighter back in his lap. He tensed, but I didn't take my hand away.

As I undid his zipper, he slowly opened his eyes and said, "I'm not..."

# Casting Couch

Tobey Field lived next door to my grandma. When I was a kid, I'd play with him in my grandma's basement on the weekends. My mom could only commit to five days of parenting a week. Tobey was the only boy who was ever my friend, not counting Abel, but I guess that's different. I don't know if Abel was my friend. I don't really know what Abel was.

Tobey never made me feel weird like every other boy did. He didn't care if I sounded like a girl and wore a tampon up my ass. I guess Tobey was different, too. But he didn't seem different, so he got away with it in a way that I never could, being the male JonBenét Ramsey and all. Well, I always did walk around like there was a tiara on my head, and everyone wanted to choke me out…

My grandma spent all her time cooking in the kitchen, so Tobey and I would hang out in the basement and watch *Mean Girls,* which I kept playing on repeat just to give my grandma something to pray about. I knew each line by heart.

One day, right when the sales lady was all like, "You could try Sears," Tobey looked over at me. I can't remember exactly how it happened, I just remember being down to our underwear and humping on the couch while my grandma was upstairs baking pies of contrition for the church.

I was pretty much in love with Tobey because he was two years older than me and had pubic hair. I always wondered how he'd end up. I'd get depressed thinking about it, as depressed as I got when wishing I were a character in one of my mom's Jackie Collins novels. I thought Tobey would probably end up getting a girl pregnant, and he'd work at the mine, same as everyone else.

Then, one weekend, I went to my grandma's, and he was gone. He'd moved across town. I saw him around sometimes after that, but he always pretended like he didn't know me. His face faded a few shades, and Tobey Field became a ghost. I thought about him a lot, though, I couldn't help it. I hated the past, but sometimes I wanted to curl up in it because at least it was familiar and safe. Sometimes I wanted life to be like *Mean Girls*; I wanted to know exactly what was going to happen right before it did.

Tobey told me what being gay meant, as if I hadn't downloaded Grindr when I was like, nine, and my mom gave me her old phone. He said that I was gay, but he wasn't because he had a girlfriend.

And then we took turns fucking each other with my Barbies.

The first person I came out to was my grade-two teacher. Her name was Mrs Schaeffer. She took me out of class because I spontaneously broke out singing Britney Spears during a test.

When she told me to "Stop that racket!" I said, "It's not racket. It's Britney, bitch."

Mrs Schaeffer didn't know what to do with me. She had already called my mom and told her she should take me to the doctor. Mom did. The doctor prescribed Ritalin for me after diagnosing me with ADHD, even though my mom said I was just an attention whore. I never did take the Ritalin; Ray got to them before I could. Mrs Schaeffer took me out in the hall and crossed her arms, looking down at me. "Every day it's the same thing, Jude. You insist on causing trouble for yourself." I tried to make myself cry because tears get you out of everything. "What's wrong with you?" she asked. I didn't know if I was supposed to answer. She looked at me, waiting.

What *was* wrong with me? Well, I never watched cartoons growing up because my mom always wanted to watch her shows: *Days of Our Lives, Gossip Girl,* and *The Real Housewives of Orange County.* What do you expect from a boy whose only role model was Blair Waldorf?

"Well?" She asked again, crossing her arms to stop herself from hitting me. "What's wrong with you?"

I looked up at her and shrugged. "I'm gay." That was what everyone else seemed to think was wrong with me.

"How do you know that word?" she gasped.

Mrs Schaeffer called my house that night. I heard the whole conversation because I was sitting next to my mom on the couch, helping her sew one of the broken straps of a sequined bra. Most kids had to vacuum once a week for allowance. Not me. I had to wipe down the latex.

"Do you have anything to tell me?" Mom asked once she'd hung up the phone.

I shook my head.

"Something you told your teacher?"

I shrugged.

She looked at me for a second and then lit a cigarette. "That Mrs Schaeffer sounds like a real bitch," she said, blowing smoke.

I told my mom a few days later. We were standing in line at Safeway when I read a headline on the front of a tabloid that said, "Kanye's Secret Shame: He's Gay!" I stared at it as we waited and kept thinking about it while we put the groceries in the trunk of the car. When we were driving home, I asked my mom, "Do you think Kanye West is gay?"

"Does taking it up the butt with your own head count?" she asked.

"Do you think it's bad to be gay?"

"What? Didn't I tell you to forget everything Father John Paul says as soon as he says it? I don't even know why I let your grandmother take you—"

"It wasn't anything Father John Paul said," I interrupted. "It was just that a magazine made it sound like a bad thing."

"What maga…Well, magazines make everything celebrities do seem like a bad thing."

"Yeah, Lindsay can't even do a line in peace."

"I know," my mom sighed. "Poor girl."

"Well, I'm gay," I said. "But I hope Kanye West isn't. Straight people can keep him."

My mom looked surprised for just a second and then she smiled. I don't think she was acting. Sometimes my mom would smile, but it was as real as her tits.

"Shocker," she said, rolling her eyes. "You've only been walking in heels better than me since you were three years old!"

## *Movie Poster*

All the girls had crushes on Mr Dawson. Alexis Crane was always squeezing her chest together, trying to give herself cleavage in front of him. He liked to start each class by reading to us for fifteen minutes. I could tell that what he liked the most was hearing his own voice. It was totally narcissistic but also kind of cute. When he read, he got so into it, you couldn't help but feel transported. Everyone else thought he was a loser because he read Jane Austen with an English accent, but I started having sex dreams about him when he asked us to write an essay on a movie that changed our lives.

I chose *The Rocky Horror Picture Show*, obviously, and even dressed as Frank-N-Furter to read my essay in front of the class. When I whipped off my cape to reveal my corset and garter belt, Matt yelled from his desk, "Go back to Transsexual, Transylvania freak!"

"What country is Transylvania in, Matt?" Mr Dawson asked, once everyone had stopped laughing.

"I don't know," Matt shrugged. "Who cares?"

"So you know more about transsexuals than geography?" Mr Dawson smirked.

Suddenly, it sounded like the room was full of owls. I'm surprised Matt didn't get up and punch Mr Dawson in the face, but for the first time, he looked embarrassed. I was never intimidated by him after that. Shame is so boring. I traced my tongue over my glistening red lips and stared straight into his eyes, arching one of my thick, illustrious brows.

"Everyone keep your mouths shut, please," Mr Dawson said. "Jude, you may continue." I kept reading with my voice shaking because the room was so quiet. I was waiting for someone to laugh every time I said a word with an "s" in it. And I couldn't have that, so I started singing, dancing on desks, shaking my ass. Soon, everyone was cheering for me. Everyone wanted a part in my movie.

When I finished, I got a standing ovation. Then the bell rang and everyone got out of the class as fast as they could. I went back to my desk and got my books. As I was about to leave, I tried to think of a way to thank Mr Dawson. That was the first time anyone had ever stood up for me, besides Angela, who usually just butted in because she liked the drama. I was worried that "thank you" would sound lame, or worse, like I was hitting on him, which was basically what every guy thought I was doing whenever I gave him a little attention. On the rare occasions I talked to Ray, he always looked at me like I'd just asked if I could give him a blow job.

I decided not to say anything at all and started to walk out of the class, but Mr Dawson stopped me. "Remember, Jude," he said, "don't dream it, be it."

As I walked out of his classroom into the hall, I imagined him slamming the door shut before I could leave. He ripped off his tie, and I fell onto his chest. His breath was hot. He was bulging. My garter belt snapped as he pulled off my necklace, pearls scattering to the floor. I ran my hand through his finger waves as he pushed me against his desk. A satin heel slipped off my foot. He pulled me onto his lap, and as my legs spread, the seam in my black underwear ripped down my ass crack which he spread open and…

I never skipped Mr Dawson's class after that. I'd skip other classes to walk around town and listen to music. I liked walking on the sidewalk, slipping on frozen dog shit, blasting Grace Jones' *Bulletproof Heart*. The only problem with skipping class too much was that, when you flunked, you had to go to summer school with all the burnouts and teen moms desperate to get on MTV.

I sat behind Luke and Madison in Mr Dawson's class. Their desks were closer together than anyone else's. I think Madison moved closer to him every class to get him stoned off her knock-off perfume and give him hand jobs under the desk when she thought no one was looking. Didn't she know there was always a paparazzi up her skirt? Of course she did. That's why she never wore underwear. I'd watch as her left arm crept under his desk, onto his lap. His ears would slowly turn red. Even if the classroom was full of voices, all I would hear was the sound of his zipper. Madison's arm moved in slow motion. She was a great Movie Star. She could really act. Sometimes she'd have an entire conversation with Alexis, who sat in the desk on the other side of her, while surreptitiously jerking Luke off. I'd chew the end of my pencil, waiting for Luke's ears to turn so red blood spilled out of them. When they did, the pencil would drop out of my hand, and my mouth would gape, saliva strung between my top and bottom lips, like his semen.

When the bell rang for lunch, I stood up and almost brought my desk with me. Angela was waiting for me at my locker.

"I'm hungry," she said, barely glancing up from her phone. "And you're late."

"You're not hungry, you just need a cigarette. And speaking of late," I smiled, touching her stomach. "Are you pregnant again?"

"Fuck you," she laughed. "I just forgot to barf my breakfast."

"I see an anonymous source has sold another story about me," I said, pointing to the "Jude Rothegay is a fudge packer" that someone had written on my locker with a Sharpie. It was fresh and shimmering, like the letters of a marquee. "They're so obsessed with me."

We bumped into Mr Callagher as we walked down the hall. He had a sadistic smirk and was slapping detention slips against his palm.

"Ah, Jude," he said when he saw me and, I swear, it was like he wanted to say Judy. "Mrs Whiltman has notified me that Glinda the Good Witch's gown for *The Wizard of Oz* is missing. Do you know anything about this?"

"No idea, Mr Callagher," I shrugged.

"Didn't you storm into my office just before winter break, complaining about casting?"

"I told you, I have to have one outburst an hour for my reality show. You know, contractual obligations. But I'd never sabotage the school production. I'm way too apathetic to care about a failed-actress-turned-junior-high-school-drama-teacher's casting decisions."

"Mrs Whiltman did cast you as the scarecrow," Mr Callagher said.

"Too bad I was auditioning for Glinda."

"We've been over this," Mr Callagher sighed. "The school wants to avoid last year's *Chicago* backlash. I'm still getting phone calls."

"Well, it was pretty stupid to cast Jude as Roxie Hart," Angela piped in. "Everyone knows he's heartless."

"And on that note," Mr Callagher said, "Mrs Whiltman has informed me you still haven't returned your costume or wig!"

"My mother mistook them for her work uniform," I said. "But I'll get them back, I promise. As soon as they're dry-cleaned..."

"And Glinda's dress?"

"Like I said, I don't know what you're talking about."

"Well, maybe an hour in detention will help you remember." He licked his lips like he enjoyed saying that a little too much. "See you at the end of the day."

"Looking forward to it," I gave him a thumbs-up, which became my middle finger when he turned his back.

The truth is, I kind of liked detention. I would pretend the detention room was my trailer and I was taking a break from the pressure of the set. It was a place where I went to learn, not just recite, my lines.

"You did take that dress, didn't you?" Angela asked as soon as Mr Callagher was out of earshot.

"Yeah," I laughed. "And those ruby hooker heels, too."

When we got back to school after lunch, I stood in the hall next to a poster for the Valentine's dance, watching Luke and Madison at their lockers. I had to stop myself from tearing down the poster. The pink, boxy font made me nauseous. Underneath the words was a picture of a big red heart. I took a marker from my backpack and drew a crack down the middle.

I tried to read Luke's lips, which were smeared with a lipstick that I wished was mine. I wanted to know what he was saying to Madison so that, when I was alone, I could imagine him saying it to me.

I was always pretending to be Madison Sinclair. I would suck in my breath to make my waist thinner and roll up my shirt, because Madison's stomach was always bare. I'd put a layer of mascara on my eyes and some ChapStick on my lips. I always felt so naked being her; she needed much less makeup than me. I'd pretend my hair was as long and blonde as hers, and so shiny that it could be in a shampoo commercial. I'd look in the mirror and move my hips the way she moved hers, like she rolled instead of walked. I wanted to be Madison because she seemed so perfect—and like such a lie. And I loved lies because, when you're a lie, you're anything, you're everything. I wanted to be Madison because I thought it would be glamorous to have a million Twitter followers. I didn't know that having it all is boring. When you have nothing, you have dreams.

Matt was standing near Luke and Madison at their lockers and caught me staring. I couldn't look away; they were French kissing. Alexis took a picture of them with her phone. They looked so flawless, the school should've blown up a picture of them kissing and put it on the Valentine's poster. A girl as deceitful as her blonde hair and a boy-next-door with charm and a hockey butt. Her eyes were wide, and his jaw was square. Her pussy was baby pink, and his ball sweat should be bottled.

Sometimes, I fantasized that my stalker had gotten to them too, tore them open from head to toe, and offered their filthy gorgeous insides to my shrine.

"Hey, Luke," Matt said, as Alexis's camera phone flashed. "Looks like your other girlfriend is getting jealous." I was so absorbed in watching them that I forgot that I could be watched, too. "Why don't you give him a kiss?" Matt laughed, and my cheeks turned red, but not as red as Luke's. "Come on, man," Matt said. "Judy's already puckering up!"

Luke looked at me, and the spotlight became so hot that I was on fire. Madison barely glanced over. She was used to me gawking at her boyfriend, and she was over it. She just looked down at Alexis's phone, telling her which photos to delete and which to tag her in.

"What's the matter?" Matt asked Luke. "He's practically a girl."

"Oh, Matt," I sighed. "Just because you want to fuck my ass like it's a pussy, doesn't make me a girl."

# Flashback

"Trey Morris," Angela said, coming up from underneath our booth with a smug look on her face.

"As if," I gasped.

"Nope, we did it last night."

"Trey Morris as in Luke Morris's brother?"

"Older and wiser, he can buy my Budweiser."

"He's your high school jock?"

"I thought you knew," she shrugged, but she knew I didn't.

"No fucking way!" I squealed. I couldn't contain myself. "Have you been over to their house?"

"Yeah. It was awkward. Luke wouldn't even look at me."

"What's he like?" I asked. "I mean, what's he *like*?"

"He's not bad."

"Big?"

"Horse."

"Balls?"

"'Roid raisins."

"Bacne?"

"I didn't want to look."

"Premature ejaculation?"

"No, but pre-come. It flowed like the Mississippi."

"Moan?"

"Grunt."

"Elvis?"

"Britney."

"Jesus!"

"But it was kind of cute. Besides, I think he's going to be quarterback next year, so I'll already have slept with the quarterback by the time I start high school."

"Does he have a girlfriend?"

"Probably."

"Well, better than a wife."

"Yeah," she took a sip from her milkshake and burped. "Or a baby."

I stabbed my hash browns with my fork, but I wasn't even hungry anymore. I had lost my appetite with jealousy. Sometimes when I looked at Angela, I got so jealous that I almost fell over. I couldn't help but think that, if I were her, I'd have everything. Or at least, everyone.

"So, are you going to take Trey to the dance?" I asked.

"As if. I don't even think I'm going unless I feel like spending the weekend e-tarded."

"Could you imagine Madison's face if you walked into the gym with Luke's *brother*? She'd die."

"On second thought, maybe I should go. Are you going?"

"Only if I can go with Luke."

"I can ask Trey to put a good word in for you."

"Right."

"I can! I have a double-jointed tongue. I'm very persuasive."

"I just can't believe you've been inside Luke's house."

"Didn't I tell you?" She smiled like she does whenever Mr Mead checks her out. "They're throwing a party this weekend 'cuz their parents are out of town. You should come."

"A party? Or a bunch of hicks drinking beer in a garage?"

"Shut up, as if you'd pass up the opportunity to get inside Luke's house."

I knew she was right. "Will he be there?" I asked.

"Probably. It's his house."

"What would he do if he saw me? What would Madison do?"

"Just don't let them see you."

"I'll never make it through the front door."

"You will if you're with me. I'll wear a low-cut shirt."

"Fine," I sighed as if I were being forced into it, even though I couldn't wait. I sensed a paparazzi ambush. "But if there's a deer's head mounted on the wall," I said, "I'm getting the hell out of there before mine ends up beside it."

After Angela left, I stayed at the Day-n-Nite to read *Pink* by Gus Van Sant, which Mr Dawson had lent me. I was obsessed with River Phoenix. I'd go over to Angela's house and we'd pop some of her mom's Percocets as we popped our popcorn, watch *My Own Private Idaho*, and swoon.

Mr Dawson always lent me the best books. Looking back, I should've known. But I honestly had no clue. It's weird when

I think about it. I see everything so differently now, it's like watching a movie for a second time and seeing all the subliminal symbols brainwashing you.

Mr Dawson's wife dropped in one time when I was eating lunch in his classroom. She knocked on the door tentatively, and he quickly stood up, ushering her in. She had hazel eyes and brown frizzy curls.

"There's someone I want you to meet," Mr Dawson told her. "You know, Jude?"

"Of course! It's so nice to finally meet you," she said, shaking my hand.

Finally? I had no idea she knew I existed.

"I'm Lisa," she beamed. "Christopher has told me so much about you." I cringed when she pointed to Mr Dawson like I couldn't figure out who she was talking about. "I think you're just great," she said, like I had asked.

I spent the rest of lunch hour trying to guess what Mr Dawson had told her about me. I wondered what tabloid version of my life he subscribed to. I wanted to know what he thought, if he knew me at all, or if I was just some unusual object he had collected. Were the little smiles he gave me from his desk genuine? Or was that just how he looked basking in my spotlight?

I didn't get through much of *Pink* before Brooke kicked me out of the Day-n-Nite for holding up the booth. I called her a philistine and then walked home. I usually tried not to go home until after dark to avoid being around Ray, but sometimes there was no escaping him or his demons.

My mom had already left for work, and Ray was on the couch

watching TV. It smelled like fast food, but that might've just been his sweat. Keefer was in his PJs, playing with Lego on his bed.

"Shouldn't you be asleep?" I asked, turning off his bedroom light.

"Hey, screw you!" he yelled. "Turn that back on."

"What did I tell you about that kind of language?"

"That it's for trashy degenerates!"

"That's right."

"But you talk like that."

"Exactly. Now get to bed. Don't you have school tomorrow?"

"I was waiting for you to read to me."

"What'd you get?"

He jumped off his bed and looked for the book in his backpack, the diary of some wimpy kid. I liked reading to Keefer. His eyes zoned out like when he played Nintendo and fell into a homicidal trance. I tried to take him out of the war zone. I always hoped that if I could give Keefer another world he could escape to, he might survive this one.

"You're not wearing nail polish," he said as I held open the book. He looked up at me with such confusion, like he never imagined my nails could be not painted. My mind flashed back to a memory of my dad like it was a pop-up advertisement. I tried to close the tab, but it was playing so loud it stunned me. The first time I'd seen him since he'd left town. I was sitting on the porch eating a popsicle. It was mid-summer; his truck drove through the gravel and stopped at the curb in front of our house. I recognized the truck before I saw him inside it, through the leafy branches reflecting on the windshield. It took him a while to get out of the truck; he just sat there staring at me.

"I thought it was you," he said, slamming the door and kicking up dust with his work boots as he walked toward me. He leaned in for a hug, but stopped. "You're wearing nail polish," he said to me, but it sounded like he was saying it to himself.

My mom was annoyed that he had just appeared out of nowhere without even calling, but when he asked to take me to the park, she said it was up to me. I said yes, even though I wanted to say no. There was something about him that made me uncomfortable.

He dug out his old baseball glove from the back of his truck and gave it to me like it was significant. I suppose it might have been, if he'd been around to teach me how to catch and throw— not that I would have made it easy for him. I could only swing my arms when I was teaching myself the choreography to a Kylie Minogue music video.

When we got back, my mom wasn't home. There was a Post-it note on the fridge for me to call her at grandma's. My dad came in the house, and I didn't know if I was supposed to let him. He asked if he could take a shower. I didn't call my mom; I just stood in the doorway of the bathroom, hoping to see a glimpse of him through the clear plastic shower curtain. I wanted to know all of him.

After his shower, he said he was going to take a nap on the couch before hitting the road again. He didn't say where he was coming from or where he was going. By the look of it, he was living in his truck. My mom called while he was sleeping; I told her dad was resting, and she let out a long sigh before asking if I was alright. I said I'd call her when he woke up. I just sat there, watching him sleep. He mumbled to himself and farted, and I was repulsed, but still inhaled it.

I wanted to crawl next to him on the couch to see if I could still fit into the curve of his arm.

## Sex Scene

I thought no one would know it was me, except I was trailing Mademoiselle like a second spirit.

I decided not to be myself for the party at Luke's house. Sometimes I had to be boring to stay alive. My goal was to blend, so before I left to meet Angela at our old elementary school playground, I put on a pair of jeans and one of Ray's grey sweaters, which I took out of the dryer.

Angela was sitting on a swing and smiled when I approached because she'd managed to get one of the drunks who sleep on the ramp outside the liquor store to go in and buy her a mickey of vodka. Usually, they run off with your money or drink the booze before they get out of the store.

"I didn't even have to flash him," she said, her cheeks red from too much blush and the cold. She passed me the bottle, and I took a quick shot.

"I'm nervous," I said.

"What's to be nervous about?" she asked, but she didn't really care. She pulled out her compact and put on more blush.

"Because I never go to parties. I'm not suicidal."

"Relax," she said, and I could tell she was irritated because all she cared about was getting laid by the teen dream and having everyone know it.

"The guys in this town are bad enough with just blood in their veins," I said, "never mind beer. I'm going to end up the next Matthew Shepard!"

"You *wish* you were that famous."

"Do I look okay?"

She looked at me for the first time.

"You look like..." She snapped her compact shut, searching for the word.

"Like?"

"A boy."

"I know," I sighed. "I feel like I should actually pee standing up."

"Kiss me," Angela suddenly demanded, smacking her wet, puffy vodka lips.

"What?"

"Kiss me. With tongue."

"What did you take from your mom's pharmacy, and why aren't you sharing?"

"I'm serious. Kiss me."

"No! I don't want to catch lip herpes."

"I don't have *lip* herpes."

"Jonathan Hampton?"

"That was a zit."

"I need a mint."

"You'll taste good," she laughed. "You'll taste like vodka."

"Do I really look like that much of a dude?"

"It's not because of how you look! I just need to know if I'm good at it."

"I'm sure your dad taught you well."

"Fuck you. Kiss me. I just want to make sure I'm good at it."

"Of course you're good at it. Amongst other things. It says so in every stall in the boys' room."

"I really like Trey, I think he could be more than just, like, you know, some thing. I think he could really be something."

"I'm sure his girlfriend agrees completely."

"She's a tramp. She has bigger boobs than me, but that's just because she's on the pill. Please?"

"Okay, fine," I shrugged. "Why not?"

I turned to face her, and we were about to do it, but I hesitated. "I've never kissed a girl," I said.

"Oh, as if! You kiss yourself in the mirror every day." She laughed and grabbed the back of my head. Before I knew it, lipstick and vodka were smeared on my lips, and her tongue was tied around mine.

"So?" She asked when we pulled away.

"You kiss like in the movies," I said, and she seemed satisfied. But it wasn't a compliment.

Angela kissed like she had to.

We left the schoolyard and walked to the party, passing the vodka bottle back and forth. When we arrived at Luke's house, Angela stopped at the front door and started talking to a couple of guys who were smoking on the steps. I crossed my arms because I thought that if I didn't, I'd jump out of my skin. I looked inside; there were so many people I could barely see past the welcome mat. Angela took my arm, and because she was jail-bait in a tube-top, the crowd parted like the Red Sea for Moses.

I spotted Luke right away. He was standing with a group of people making a pyramid out of beer cans on the kitchen counter. When I turned to say something to Angela, she was gone—probably already in one of the bedrooms. Some drunk girl I had never seen before hugged me like we were best friends and gave me her beer before stumbling off. It was mostly spit, but I drank it anyway. I didn't want Luke to see me so I went down to the basement where the stoners were sitting around the couch taking bong hoots while *Labyrinth* played silently on the TV. Even Hoggle was killing fairies. I finished the beer standing against the wall like a flower, trying not to think of Luke, because the last thing I needed was to be a flower with a stem. I already wanted to leave the party, but I couldn't move, so I watched David Bowie light up the big screen like a glitter god. Although he had nothing on Jobriath.

Alexis came out of the bathroom with a couple of girls acting more coked out than they really were. They started dirty dancing. Alexis threw her head back and forth like she was filming a music video on YouTube that would ask you to prove your age before you could view it. She gave me a dirty look and laughed with her friends, who were all wearing the same American Apparel tank tops in different colours.

I had to get out of there, the set was haunted. The party was unbearable. I went to find Angela and tell her that I was leaving, or else needed all of her mom's dolls so that I could at least pretend I was Jareth. It had been a mistake for me to come. This trashy teen drama wasn't challenging enough. I was a true actor, an artist. Not just some coked-out Disney princess with an Electra complex. *Vanity Fair* even said so.

While I was looking for Angela, I noticed Luke's family portrait hanging on the wall. You could tell his dad probably looked just like Luke and Trey when he was younger. They all seemed like they could throw a ball really far, enjoyed having their asses rimmed, and know how to skin a deer. Just then, Luke walked past without seeing me and sat on the couch. Madison stumbled over and fell into his lap. He put his arm around her, and her head rolled into the curve of his armpit, her blonde hair falling over her face.

All I wanted was for Luke to acknowledge me, because he never would. I'd only get his attention if I demanded it like a hysterical fan trying to touch him just to prove he was alive.

Madison gave him a sloppy kiss. Luke put his hand on her back, covering the tramp-stamp of a lily sticking out from underneath her tank top. When he pulled away, Luke looked up and almost saw me, but I dodged for the stairs.

I looked for Angela in the bathroom, but there was just a dude passed out in the bathtub with a beer tucked under his arm. Someone had turned on the shower, and water was pouring over him, washing away the puke. I looked in the master bedroom, but there were two-and-a-half people having sex on

Luke's parents' bed. I mean, the girl didn't look fully conscious.

I heard moaning coming from one of the rooms, so I put my ear to the door. It was Angela. I'd recognize that sound anywhere. It was just like that time she got alcohol poisoning. I was about to leave, but right next to Trey's room was what had to be Luke's bedroom door. I opened it, expecting to see someone inside, but it was empty. The room was dark and smelled like laundry detergent and Adidas cologne and his hair when it's sweaty, like right after gym class. I stepped in without thinking, and the door closed behind me. The window was open just a crack; the room was colder than the rest of the house. I could hear screaming outside. Someone had thrown a beer bottle instead of a snowball.

I went to his bed and turned on the nightstand lamp. He had a couple *Sports Illustrated* magazines in his drawer, some condoms, a guitar pick, loose change, a Snickers wrapper, and a picture of him and his brother posing next to a dead moose with rifles at their feet. Right next to the picture lay a piece of paper rolled up in an elastic band. I listened for footsteps, but I could only hear the bass of the rap music pounding through the floor.

I unrolled the paper—it was a target. There were bullet holes through the centre that were so small, I couldn't even fit my little finger through them. As I rolled it back up, I noticed an elementary school picture in the drawer. On the back, in messy printing, he'd written, "Luke Morris, Grade 1." I pocketed the photo, then ran my hands across his bed and pressed my face against the sheets. They were wrinkled and covered with come stains. I was tempted to lick one, but I heard laughing from the hallway and barely had time to flick off the lamp before I saw shadows at the bottom of the door.

I jumped into the closet right as the door opened. Luke walked in carrying Madison. I could see them through the slits in the closet door. He didn't turn on the lights but moved through the dark and dropped her on the bed. He took off his shirt and climbed on top of her. The music downstairs was blaring so loudly, I was surprised the cops hadn't shown up. Madison began to groan like she liked the way it hurt. And I kept watching because maybe I liked it, too. The bed started to squeak. I watched Luke's body as he went into her, but it wasn't like in my dreams. He started breathing heavier, but I couldn't hear it over the music; I could just see it in the way his body moved. I clasped my hands together to stop from touching myself.

When they were done, he got up right away and put his shirt back on, then looked around for his hat. He turned on the lamp and found it sticking out from under the bed. His face was red, and his hair was stuck to his forehead. Suddenly, the music stopped; I didn't let myself breathe. Madison curled up on the bed with her blonde hair cascading in waves over the side.

"Turn off the light," she moaned.

He flicked the switch, and everything was dark again.

"The music stopped," she said.

"Yeah." He adjusted his hat and looked right at me—right at the slits in his closet door. "Are you going to pass out?" he asked, running his hand through her sea of hair.

"Luke?" she said in her baby voice, which I imitated when I was alone in my room.

"Yeah?"

"Do you love me?" she asked, and it's a good thing the music started again because I almost choked. I don't know what he said or if he said anything at all. She got up. I was glad it was dark and that I couldn't see. I didn't want to see her lipstick all over him, on his lips, his neck, his eyelids.

When they opened the door, the room filled with light, and the music got even louder. I fell back into his dirty laundry in the closet. I wanted the smell to stay on me forever. I wanted to bottle it. I wanted it to be my signature scent. Dirty. Strong. *Unforgettable.* I waited a while, then came out of the closet and stood next to his bed. The blanket was bunched, and the sheets were damp. I touched them even though they made my hands feel like they were on fire.

I didn't care if anyone in the hallway saw me: I walked right out. I didn't even care if Luke and Madison were standing there, their faces still shining. I didn't care about anything. I walked down the stairs almost tripping over my laces. I was wearing the most normal shoes I owned. My grandma bought them for me for Christmas. They were purple. She wrote "Love, Santa" on the box because that's what she always did. She wouldn't let me thank her for them either; it was really important to her that I believed.

I decided to go out the back door because there was a big crowd at the front, and I didn't want to deal with it. I wasn't in the mood to be harassed by the fans. They always expected so much from me. I could see my breath in the air, maybe because it was so cold outside or maybe because I was so cold inside. Three guys were standing in the backyard, all wearing the bro-army uniform of hoodies, baseball caps, blue jeans, and sneakers. One of them was taking a piss on the fence, and the other two were drinking beer and sharing a joint. They stopped talking when they saw me. One squinted his eyes and the other laughed.

"What the fuck are you?" he asked.

He said it with such awe, it was almost flattering. I didn't stop to wonder what it was about me that they saw. I had tried to look like everyone else, but maybe it was written all over my face. I kept walking. There was dog shit on the path. I told myself not to step in it, but I did anyway. It was like I stepped in it because I told myself not to. It was fresh, not yet frozen, and I felt it squish under my foot.

"Hey, Brian, I think this fag wants to watch you piss. You want to see his cock, faggot?"

Maybe it was my fury over stepping in dog shit that made me lunge at him. Or maybe it was that I did indeed want to watch Brian piss. In fact, I wanted him to piss in my mouth. I wanted to drink it. Instead, I decided to drink blood and clawed at the guy's face, but didn't get to do any real damage before he punched my nose, and I flew backward into the snow, miraculously missing the dog shit. The other two came after me, but I quickly got on my feet. Blood dripped from my nose, giving me red geisha lips.

I didn't feel the pain. I just felt the silk kimono that in my head I was wearing, with its obi trailing behind me as I ran. The wind whistling in my ears was like the strings of the shamisen. I was running for my life, but in my mind I was dancing like I was available for the night.

## *Train Wreck*

All the lights were off in the house when I got home, but I could see the glare from the TV flashing through the front window, lighting up Ray as he sat on the couch. I stood on the sidewalk, catching my breath, tasting blood, coming in and out of focus as the snow blew off the tree branches onto my head.

When I walked through the front door, Ray was watching TV in the living room. Keefer was asleep on the floor, curled up without a blanket and sucking his thumb like he would sometimes, even though Ray always slapped his hand out of his mouth. My mom was at work, which is why Keefer wasn't in bed; Ray always let Keefer fall asleep in front of the TV, just like he let him watch TV sitting so close that you could see his breath on the screen. As if Keef wasn't brain damaged enough. My mom didn't show until she was nearly five months pregnant, so she kept dancing. All that spinning, who could blame him for being special.

I intended to go straight down to my room because I didn't

want Ray to see my face, but I knew he'd let Keef stay there all night, so I bent down to pick him up off the floor.

"He's fine," Ray said, shifting his body because I was blocking the screen. I heard him crunching Doritos under his ass. "Leave him alone."

I picked Keefer up anyway and took him to his room. He didn't wake up. That kid could sleep through anything, which was definitely his saving grace. I lay him in his bed and put the covers over him. There were toys everywhere, and his sheets were on the floor because he'd been trying to make a tent. I told him that I'd help, but I never did.

Ray was standing next to the basement door when I walked out of Keef's room. I felt drunk just from smelling him. You could tell Ray had been really good-looking in high school—tall, dark, and bad. You could also tell that he still thought he was good looking. But his baby blues weren't as irresistible when they couldn't even focus.

"I said he was fine," Ray said, blocking the doorway. "You just don't listen, do you? You always have to fuss with him." He took his calloused hand and grabbed my chin, lifting my nose to the hallway light. "What the hell happened?"

"Don't touch me," I said, trying to pull away.

"Someone put you in your place?" he asked, laughing.

"I deserved it, huh?"

"Your words," he said, stepping away from the door. "Not mine."

I went down to my room and sat on the edge of my bed, listening to the floorboards creak as Ray walked to the bathroom. If I had really strained myself, I probably could've heard him scratching his balls. Then, more creaking as he walked back to the living room, rocking the floor as he sat down on the couch. He turned the volume on the TV so high that I could hear all the bad jokes on *SNL*.

I ignored Stoned Hairspray, who was trying to get me to pet her, grabbed *Breakfast at Tiffany's* off my bookshelf, and opened it to the back page where I kept a razor blade tucked behind the dust jacket. Angela gave it to me; she carried razors in her clutch like they were cherry ChapSticks. I never went too deep—I was too vain. I just dragged the blade down my forearm, pulling the tiny blonde hairs, then across my wrist, digging for blood diamonds.

I fell asleep on Stoned, who was used to being my pillow. I think she knew how much I needed her. She was the only one who didn't sell stories about me, and even if it was just because she couldn't talk, I loved her for it. She let me cry into her fur, and when I woke up, she was still wet, as if I had kept crying in my sleep.

I picked a glob of blood out of my nose. My face was swollen, and it was kind of hard to breathe, but I didn't miss my sense of smell because I generally had to throw bottles of perfume against the cement walls just to get rid of the basement's musty odour, and because I liked to pretend the walls were my personal assistants.

I tried to cover the bruising on my nose with makeup, but it was still obvious. I kept staring at my face in the mirror. There was something about black and blue that made me feel like, well, such a man. It was a whole new role for me to play.

I didn't want to face everyone upstairs. I could smell the French toast my mom was making. Every once in a while, she decided to be domestic, but it never worked out; she always burned something or gave someone food poisoning. The thing with my family was that we always seemed the most abnormal when we were doing the normal things.

I put on my biggest pair of Jackie O sunglasses and escaped through the window, texting Angela to meet me at the Day-n-Nite. When I got there, I sat in the back booth waiting for her. I kept my glasses on. I was so famous I had to go incognito.

Brooke came over, but I didn't order anything, I didn't have any money. She brought me a cup of coffee anyway. Brooke could be good like that sometimes. I always wondered about her name. She just didn't look like a Brooke. You never think a Brooke is going to be some fatty whose neck folds remind you of a vagina. You don't think of a fifty-year-old waitress who looks like she's never been to the dentist. You think of a Brooke as some blonde bitch in L.A. with perky tits and a phony personality, someone with a white dog named Snowball and a husband who buys her jewellery every time he cheats on her. Someone living the dream life.

Angela was late again, so I looked out of the window at the smoke billowing over the mine. I caught a trucker staring at me through the reflection. He sat at the counter, and I turned to look at him. He smiled, chewing a burger with his mouth open. He wore a hat and a long-sleeved flannel shirt that looked like it had never been washed. Typical Day-n-Nite trucker. He stared at me, and I let him. I don't know if he thought I was a boy or a girl or if he even cared. I slowly took off my sunglasses and stared back into his beady eyes, looking him up and down, licking my lips. His smile got so big that I could see his cavities. He was practically panting. I started thinking about some porno my mom caught me jerking off to once, one with a perverted truck driver and some dazed and confused hitchhiker. My pants got tighter, and I felt so disgusted with myself that you'd think I'd eaten my mom's French toast. The trucker's smile got even bigger as he poked his tongue in his cheek, and his hands disappeared beneath the counter. I picked up my glass of water and started sucking on the straw, slipping my lips down it inch by inch until my eyes started to water. His face got red and blotchy, like he was almost there. I bit my chipped nails as he rubbed his palms on his jeans and panted.

Then I saw Angela through the window and jumped out of the booth, knocking into the table and spilling coffee over the edge of my cup. I air-kissed the trucker as I walked past, like he was a fan. I put my glasses back on and stopped Angela before she came through the door. The trucker spun around so fast to see me leave that he almost broke the seat.

"Where are we going?" Angela asked, pulling her arm away as I dragged her down the street. "I'm hungry!"

"I have no money," I said. "I tried to steal some of my mom's tips, but she was too busy playing housewife for me to get a chance."

"Fuck it," she sighed, "I have booze bloat. I shouldn't eat anything anyway." Angela pulled her phone from her purse to check a text and asked me, "Do you know Mikey K?"

"The dealer?"

"Yeah, Mike Johnson. His mom's a vet. He has the best Special K."

"I prefer Cheerios."

"He's at the mall. We can meet him."

"I don't like Mikey. He poured a can of Pepsi over my head once."

"Yeah, because you told him you wanted to have sex with his dad."

"Whatever. He's an asshole."

"So forget the asshole," she smiled, crossing the street to the bus stop. "And fall into a K-hole."

When the bus came, we sat at the back near a homeless man and some boys who were a few years older than Keef and a few years short of a criminal record. They stared at me for the entire ride, like I was some exotic animal at the zoo. I didn't know whether to growl or start signing autographs. Angela didn't say anything about my nose. I don't think she noticed. Angela didn't notice anything except missed periods and how many Likes she was getting on Facebook.

We met Mikey K in the mall food court by the photo booths. He was wearing a baseball cap backward, and his jeans were so low on his hips that his ass was hanging out. He had on Bart Simpson boxers, and when I said, "Oh my God, are those Jeremy Scott?" he looked at me like I wasn't speaking English. Angela hugged him, and he put his hand on her lower back. I tried to remember if his name was written under the table at our booth. He nodded his head at me, the way some guys do instead of actu-ally speaking, and tried to shake my hand. But I couldn't do the handshake—I could never do them. On the rare occasion that someone was willing to touch my hand, I'd always end up embarrassing myself. I don't know why Mikey even tried. I guess because I was a client and everything, but he was still kind of awkward, like he was worried I wouldn't let his hand go.

"So what do you have?" Angela asked.

"We're thinking of trying K," I said.

"I won't have any K until career day."

"But you're Mikey *K*," Angela whined, like she didn't believe him, like she thought he was keeping it all to himself.

"So what do you have?" I asked.

"Just some bud and a couple hits of acid."

"Acid!"

"Acid?"

"Five bucks a hit," he said.

"I have twenty bucks," Angela said, pulling her makeup and cigarettes out of her purse to find the bill.

They went into the photo booth to do the exchange and were in there for so long that I wondered what else they were doing. I stood awkwardly looking out at the food court until Mikey finally came out. "Later, mang," he said as he passed me, his jeans even lower.

Angela and I went into the handicapped bathroom which we used to hot-box in all the time when Angela was being a monk or whatever and always wanted to get high and chant Hare Krishnas. She claimed the handicap bathroom at the mall had really good energy, at least when the pregnancy tests she took in it were negative.

"Sink or sin," Angela said as we took the acid. We stuck out our tongues and stared at our reflections in the finger-smudged mirror. The stamps had pictures of an eternity symbol on them, and we each took two. I could feel them dissolving into my spit. Angela took out her iPhone and stuck out her tongue as the camera flashed.

It didn't take long for everything to start to change. It was like the bathroom lights were flicking on and off by themselves. I turned on the tap, and the water was so hot that the skin on my hands turned red and peeled, but I couldn't stop shivering. Angela spun around with both of her arms sticking out like fallen-angel wings, her feathers scraping against the wall and knocking off plaster. I picked up the crumblings and rubbed them on my face like they were mother-of-pearl.

We played music off Angela's phone, and the bass felt like universes colliding. There was this pervasive boom coming from all around, or maybe from within. We both stood there looking at our reflections, stuck in the beat, our eyes slowly drooping and turning black. It was like we were purely animal. We had no souls.

When the song ended, the boom kept echoing. The colour returned to Angela's eyes first, and she grabbed my arm, resurrecting me with a gasp. Angela pointed to the door, and I realized someone was knocking. "Mall cop," she whispered.

The booming stopped, and we heard keys jingling like my mom's bangles on my wrists, sliding across my scars and catching on my scabs. When the door opened, the mall cop's moustache was turned up like horns.

"How many times do I have to tell you fucking kids?" He screamed. "It is rude to rave in the handicap bathroom!"

We rushed past him and ran, but for once, it wasn't just like the movies—he didn't chase us, and there wasn't a frenzied sequence of running through the mall, jumping over strollers, pushing grannies off the escalator, and shoplifting along the way. He just stood there and watched us go, clutching the cell-phone attached to his belt loop like a gun.

We ran into Wal-Mart where all the smiley faces jumped off the discount signs and bounced on the floor like rubber balls. Water spilled out of the candy aisle, followed by a tsunami of chocolate.

We swam past the cocked firearms, which had grown their own arms and were jerking their load. When they started to fire, we dove under the surface, but then everything started to dry up, and shoppers were getting shot, splitting like a two-for-one discount. The mirrors started to bleed. Someone had summoned Bloody Mary.

"Mommy," Angela said, holding one of the cashiers at gun-point with a rifle and emptying a cash register into her purse. The fluorescent lights flickered through my rapid blinks. The blood from the mirrors spilled onto the floor and made the candy water red.

I trudged through body parts to the meat freezer and picked up a package of steaks. My face was reflected in the light shining off the tight plastic wrap. I was suffocating. As I watched, my skin dissolved until I was just a skull. My mouth opened and I screamed, but no sound came out. The package filled with blood, which pushed against the plastic until it burst and spilled over my hands. Soon the freezer overflowed, and even the walls started to bleed. I tried to move, but the blood at my feet was so thick, it was like running in a slow-motion dream. I pinched myself but didn't wake up.

When I opened my eyes, I was out of breath from running. We were in the schoolyard, and both of our wrists were bleeding. Angela was spinning around with her arms out, making red rain that stuck to my skin. When it dried, I felt like I had been dipped in candle wax.

We dropped to the ground and made snow angels with bloody wings. I rested my head on her shoulder and she held my hand. The sun shone through the cloud of smoke from the mine, shooting toxic rays of light.

"Darling," she said, "we're a train wreck."

"Sweetheart," I said, "train wrecks always make the front page."

# Sunset Boulevard

I woke up the next morning and rolled to my side, facing my tattered Marilyn picture. I thought my eyes were playing tricks on me, like I was still tripping or something, because there was a tear streaking down her face. It took me a minute to realize that I'd left my window open and melted snow had dripped onto the picture. The tear fit, somehow, like it had always been there. Like the photo was taken right after she'd been raped by a studio exec.

A glance in the mirror showed me that I looked like my mom when she came home from work, her makeup worn off with sweat and dark circles under her misty eyes. I used to wake up every morning when she came home. I'd hear the door creak open and slip out of bed to make sure that it was her. I knew that it would be, but I still had to check. She started to leave me alone some nights, before Ray moved in and Keef was born. Usually Ray would crash at our place, but if he pulled a Houdini, she'd have no choice. She never told me, but I'd wake up, and the house would be empty. I would get out of bed and make sure the door was locked and then crawl under my covers. It would take forever to fall back asleep because every noise would scare me. I usually just stayed awake until I heard her come home. As soon as she walked in, she would flop down on the couch, exhausted. I'd get out of bed and cuddle next to her. She'd run her acrylic nails through my hair, and I'd rest my head on her shoulder, which always smelled like beer and perfume.

"Did you hit the jackpot?" I'd ask, because sometimes we would pretend that she was a Vegas showgirl and we lived in the penthouse of The Mirage.

"They tip me like I'm Nomi Malone," she said, resting her head against mine, "even when I try to be Martha Graham."

As I was watching the drop of water slide down Marilyn's cheek, I remembered I had a joint somewhere and ransacked my nightstand drawer to find it. I got Stoned stoned with me by blowing smoke in her face. She could be so petulant when I didn't share.

Once I was high, I showered and dragged myself to school for second period, which was gym. Angela wasn't around (her Twitter said she was at Trey's "consummating and watching *Girls*"), so I had to sit on the sidelines alone in gym.

When I started to feel too exposed to the paparazzi, I ducked into the change room. I checked out my reflection in one of the mirrors before finding a stall to hide out in. The swelling had gone down on my nose, but I was convinced that it was crooked and that I'd need a nose job, which I was kind of excited about because I was sure it'd get me tons of press.

I lit the roach of the joint I'd smoked earlier as the change room door opened and someone walked in, catching their breath. I looked through the crack in the stall and saw Luke go to one of the urinals. I dropped the roach into the toilet bowl, and he turned his head when it sizzled.

"Who's blazing?" he asked, flushing and then walking over to the sink to wash his hands. He checked himself out in the mirror, his lips pouting like a reflex, then turned to look at the stalls. "Who's in there?" he asked, drying his hands on his sweaty shirt. I didn't answer, so he pushed all the stalls open one by one, and when he came to the one I was in, he flung it open because the lock was busted. "Oh," he said when he saw me backed against the wall. "It's just you."

"Just me," I nodded.

"Why didn't you say something? Worried I'd mistake you for a chick?"

He didn't wait for me to answer. He just shook his shaggy head and pulled out his phone from his gym bag. He knew I was watching him, and he held his phone so hard I thought it might break. He looked up at me like he was about to say something, but changed his mind. I wanted him to say something. Even if he just called me a fag, especially if he called me a fag. I wanted him to say it with spit flicking off his bottom lip straight onto my tongue.

"I like your shorts," I said as he put his phone back. "Are they new?"

"Stop looking at my shorts," he said, slamming the locker door shut.

"All I said was that I like them," I shrugged. "Then again, maybe I just like what's in them."

"What's your fucking problem?" he asked.

"That I'm not fucking you."

He took a step forward like he was about to knock me out, and I bit my lip because I wanted him to. I wanted him to touch me, even if it meant that my nose would get more deformed. All the best celebrities have had at least three nose jobs. But he stopped himself, brushing past me.

"You never learn," he said. "Do you?"

At lunch, I went to Mr Dawson's class because Angela was still ditching and I wanted some company. Sometimes he seemed even lonelier than me. I could see it in his eyes. Mr Dawson was always looking at me. I'd be sitting at my desk, working on an essay or something, and I'd suddenly feel like I was trapped behind a screen only to look up and find Mr Dawson fogging it.

When I caught him staring, I was never sure if he was really looking at me. His eyes sort of glazed over, and he seemed a million miles away. When he snapped back to reality, he'd meet my eye and sometimes seem surprised to see me staring back at him. He usually gave me a little smile or wink, but sometimes he did neither. He was lost in the fog.

As we ate lunch, I told him all about how I was going to move to Hollywood and be a prostitute.

"I thought you want to be a movie star?" Mr Dawson asked.

"Same thing," I shrugged.

"Well, you definitely have star quality," he said, and then blushed from the underlying implication. I could tell he wanted to reach for his wallet to see if he could afford me.

"I do have star quality," I told him, spreading my legs. "And everyone's already always talking shit about me, so I might as well get paid for it."

Mr Dawson laughed so hard that he choked on his coffee, spilling some on his tie. "I should run this under water before the stain sets," he said, getting up from his desk and walking to the door, but he stopped as Luke walked passed in the hall. "Oh, Mr Morris," Mr Dawson called out to him, "I'm still waiting for your *Romeo and Juliet* essay. You're failing without it. I expect you in my classroom at the end of the day."

"Can't today, Mr D," Luke said, not even glancing at me as I stared at him from behind Mr Dawson. "I'm going to the shooting range with my dad."

"Then have it on my desk by tomorrow. If you can find time for target practice, you can find time to write a thousand words." Luke nodded automatically, like Mr Dawson was some bitch telling him not to come inside her because she isn't on the pill. "You could always ask Jude here for some tutoring," Mr Dawson told Luke, who froze. I watched as his ears turned red and then stared at his crotch, waiting for a jiz stain to appear. "Not only did he hand his essay in on time, but he got an A."

"Yeah, Luke," I smiled at him from behind Mr Dawson. "I wouldn't mind helping you. For a price."

He looked right at me, but his expression was blank. The colour of his ears went back to normal and his cheeks didn't blush, so I felt like a total failure. I was losing my charm. I thought he might say something, but he quickly looked away, like he was afraid if I got into his head he'd never be able to get me out.

I didn't tell Mr Dawson that I had a crush on Luke, but he knew. Everyone did. Luke, Madison, and I were our school's top celebrity love triangle. We were always trending, and *everyone* followed.

"You know, Jude," Mr Dawson said once Luke had walked off, his voice suddenly softer as he faced me from the doorway, "there's something I hope you always remember, especially when you're trying to make it big in Tinseltown."

"Always get the money first?"

"That it's better to be hated for who you are than loved for who you're not."

By the time I left school at the end of the day, the sun was setting because I'd had to stay late for detention. I always got detention. I was touching up my makeup during biology and, one by one, everyone turned to stare. I think it made Mr Hudgens jealous. But, really, no one gives a fuck about how their Big Mac is digested.

As I walked home, I tried to turn the bungalows into Beverly Hills mansions, but I couldn't. No matter how hard I tried, they remained houses with chipped and peeling paint, buried in snow. It really scared me that I couldn't even dream it. But then there was a voice in my head. I heard it so clearly that I stopped in the middle of the street and looked behind me to see if anyone was there. But it was just the voice, like a prompter reminding me of my line from off stage.

Be it.

I walked through the parking lot of a Blockbuster that had

100

closed down months before, but no new business had opened. Someone had spray-painted the sign so that it read *Bye*buster. I didn't want it to go. I had walked through that parking lot so many times and seen the empty shelves and the fluorescent lights in the vacant store, which for some reason were always on, that I just got used to the emptiness. I started to get scared of what might take its place. The longer the Blockbuster contained only movie star ghosts, the more I started to believe that the emptiness was meant to last forever.

From the parking lot I ran the rest of the way home, not stopping until I walked through the front door of my house. I knew what I had to do, and I wasn't going to wait because, if I did, eventually the emptiness wouldn't scare me anymore. It would just be there like it always had been, like it was all there ever was.

Ray was working, Keefer was at a friend's house, and my mom was in bed sleeping. I stood outside her bedroom door listening for the sounds of her snores, and when I was sure she was asleep, I slowly crept in. The door made noise, but didn't wake her. Her shoes were bulging out of the closet and there were red lipstick notes on the mirror above her dresser for her hair appointment, Keefer's parent/teacher meeting, a list of groceries. She always wrote things on the mirror because she "never forgot to look in it."

She was lying with her head on her arm, her long dark hair spilling over the side of the bed. She kept all her cash on top of her dresser tied with hair elastics, next to her bottles of nail polish and a framed picture of me and Keef.

I only had to take a couple steps into the bedroom to be able to reach the dresser. I kept my eyes on her face for any sign of consciousness as I glided across the floor. She didn't budge. I picked up a stack of bills, rolled the elastic off, and pocketed a quarter of them.

When I got back down to the basement, I counted. I had twenty-seven bucks, all in singles. I put them in a shoebox and hid it under my bed. I was shaking like I was going through withdrawal, like it had been five minutes since someone had taken my picture. I was nervous and excited because for the first time, I had hope. It seemed possible, like I could do it. Maybe not with only twenty-seven bucks, but it was a start. Besides, I had read in a Madonna biography that she moved to New York with thirty-five dollars in her pocket and somehow, things worked out for her. And keep in mind, she had hairy armpits back then. If that doesn't prove that anything is possible, I don't know what does.

I couldn't wait to not have to try to imagine that the defunct Blockbuster was the Paramount Pictures lot or that the "2 for 1" sign in the discount store on Main Street was a billboard on Rodeo Drive. I wouldn't have to pretend that every time I sat in the park with Abel, I was having a lunch at The Ivy. I wouldn't have to squint my eyes to fool myself into seeing the Hollywood sign on top of a mountain of snow. If I were there, it would be real. I would be real.

Finally.

# *Shoot-out*

"I just don't get it," Angela said, flipping through a magazine and puffing on a cigarette as she sat on her parents' bed with a box of their sex toys and porn. "Which one of them is into this stuff?"

"I'm guessing the pink wig is for your father," I said, striking a pose in front of the full-length mirror in Mrs Adams' wedding dress. "He is balding."

"But what about what's in this magazine?" She held up a picture of three cartoon animals going at it. "Which one of them is a furry?"

"Okay, call me a slut, but I would totally do that fox."

"You're a creep."

I took another shot of the Sourpuss we stole from the liquor cabinet.

"Oh come on, like you wouldn't."

"Like you would," she said, flicking her cigarette ash over the side of the bed. "You're the one who's still a virgin."

"I can't help it. I'm far too in love with myself to love anyone else."

"That's as transparent as saying you're celibate by choice."

"Well, I'm saving myself for Zac Efron."

"Get over it, Jude. He's not gay. That picture was a hoax."

"He wouldn't be able to resist me."

"You're going to die alone and miserable if you keep going after straight guys."

"Says the girl who will have screwed and screwed over every guy in this town by graduation."

"Do you think that's why they went away for the weekend? So they could put on costumes and do it like animals?"

"Probably. I just can't believe your mom wore white."

"I'm not even drunk," Angela sighed, taking another shot. "And I need to be drunk for this."

"Well, I suddenly have an urge to roll on the floor and sing, 'Like A Virgin,' so I would say I'm…perfectly sober."

"There might be enough vodka in the vodka bottle filled with water to catch a buzz."

"I'll go get it," I said, winking. "I know you're dying to try The Shake-Spear."

I stepped into the hallway just as Abel's girlfriend Carly was coming out of the bathroom.

"Nice dress," she said, but her voice was flat, so I couldn't tell how she meant it. I had never seen her in person before, only the picture Abel kept in his wallet. She had light brown hair, but I bet she put "blonde" on her driver's license. Her skin was smooth, and she had light freckles on her nose. Her liquid eyeliner was smudged in the corners, like she and Abel had just been doing it. I looked at her and ached.

Abel came out of his room shirtless, and that's when I realized that Carly was wearing his shirt, a blue button-up that was too big for her. She wasn't wearing pants. Her legs were smooth and chalk white. We were all pasty; it had been a long winter. The sun only shone on TV.

"Your mother has great taste, Abel," I said, doing a spin. "You like?"

"Sure," he shrugged, scratching his bare chest, which was turning as red as his face. I couldn't stop staring at his fuzzy blond treasure trail.

"Who wants to play Russian roulette?" Angela asked, stumbling out of her parents' bedroom. The pink wig was crooked on her head, covering one of her eyes. She dangled a black gun from her middle finger.

"Where the hell'd you find that?" Abel asked.

"Underneath Mom and Dad's mattress," she shrugged. "They hide things there too."

"You should've left it," Abel said.

"Relax, loser. It's not even loaded."

"Why do your parents have a gun?" I asked.

"Why wouldn't they?" Carly said.

"Yours don't?" Abel asked.

"See," Angela said, putting the gun in her mouth.

"Angela, cut the shit!"

She pulled the trigger and it clicked. Then she started giving the barrel fellatio. Carly rolled her eyes and looked away while I cheered her on.

"Give it to me, you ho-bag," Abel demanded, grabbing it out of her mouth. He aimed it at her head and pulled the trigger—it clicked. Then, he spun around like he was 007 and fired. I screamed as the gun went off, shattering the window at the end of the hall. It was so fast that, at first, I didn't know what happened. But then Abel dropped the gun, and Carly jumped back like she was scared it might go off again. She stepped on the train of Mrs Adams's wedding dress, which ripped.

"Jesus Christ," Abel gasped. "I thought you said it wasn't loaded!"

"Well, not entirely," Angela laughed. "How else are we going to play Russian roulette?"

I stared at the gun, then slowly picked it up. It was heavier than I thought. I guess I expected it to be as light as a toy because that's what it looked like. It was so cold, I was surprised Angela's lips hadn't gotten stuck around it.

Angela put on some music and Abel yelled for her to turn it down, but she couldn't hear over the bass. He started putting cardboard on the broken window and Carly swept up the shattered glass. I put the gun to my temple.

I was born with a cunt in my brain. I was fucked in the head.

Angela came over and took the gun out of my hand, kissing my cheek. She was holding a bottle of wine she'd found hidden at the back of her parents' closet like they were saving it for a special occasion. "Come take a bath with me," she said in her baby voice that no boy could resist, not even me.

Mrs Adams' veil dripped over the edge of the bubble bath as we got in the water. At least Angela didn't make me get naked like last time or pee and then take a mouthful of water, squirting it in my face and shrieking with laughter.

As the bathroom mirror steamed up and we sat across from each other in the tub, I decided I should tell her that I was leaving, even if I was scared that she'd beg me to stay. Or maybe that she wouldn't.

"I'm getting the hell out of here," I said.

"Why? The water's still warm."

"Not the bath. This town."

"Well, yeah," she said. "Who isn't?"

I didn't say anything, but I knew that she'd never get out. That she'd have her first kid by senior year, be a beauty school dropout, have the couch in the police station named after her, and live unhappily ever after with her very own Ray, her French-tip nails wrapped around a bottle of booze.

"No," I said, "I mean I'm leaving soon. I'm saving up for a bus ticket."

"What do you mean?" She asked. "A bus ticket where?"

"Hollywood."

"Okay," she laughed.

"I'm serious, Angela. I have to get out."

She took a big swig from the wine bottle, letting it dribble down her chin into the bubbles. She was waiting for me to crack up and looked so wasted, her eyes reminded me of Stoned Hairspray when she'd stare off like she could see my demons.

"I can't stay here anymore," I told her. "I'll die."

She just kept looking at me, waiting. But when I didn't laugh, didn't even smile, she took off her pink wig and dropped it to the wet tile floor.

"When?"

"As soon as I can steal enough money from my mom. Her new boobs are bringing in a fortune so it shouldn't be too long."

She nodded, chugged the wine.

"So, what—you think you're going to go to Hollywood and be a starlet or something?"

"Well, why not? I'm already tragic enough, and I love pills and champagne."

"Yeah, but you won't sleep with anyone," she said. "You won't sleep with *everyone*. How do you expect to get cast in anything?"

"That's why you should come with me."

"No," she said, grabbing a handful of bubbles and holding them in her palm, blowing lightly until they separated and drifted between us. "I can't come with you." At least Angela knew it.

"It's my dream," I said.

"You'll be back," she said.

I shook my head once, slowly.

She nodded, smiling so prettily I almost believed it was real. "Well," she sighed, emptying the rest of the wine into our bathwater, turning it red and staining Mrs Adams's wedding gown, "here's to your dream."

"It looks like we're soaking in blood," I laughed.

"Yours," Angela said, dropping the bottle with a splash.

When I got out of the bath and dried off, Angela was already curled up in her bed. Her sheets were soaked all around her. She had passed out on the far side so she wouldn't sleep clutching my arm like a teddy bear the way she usually did.

I knew I wasn't going to be able to sleep, so I just sat on the edge of the bed looking down at her. She looked like a blow-up doll. White skin and pink lips. Her mouth was open, and there was a little drool hanging from the corner of her mouth, but she was still beautiful. Angela was the most beautiful girl I knew. She wasn't generic like Madison and Alexis. They were beautiful, I guess, but their beauty was cheap. Anyone with a fake tan who wasn't afraid of a nip-slip could look like them.

I looked up at the Bob Marley poster above Angela's bed, which I could sort of make out in the dark. Her dad had ripped it off her wall once in a rage after he'd "confiscated" her pipe. She'd cried because she really loved that pipe. We called it Liberace, partly because it was so sparkly and partly because Angela used it as an anal dildo. I helped her tape the poster and put it back on the wall. Bob was smoking a blunt and smoke streamed off his lips. "Is this love?" was written on the bottom.

I decided to walk home. I took off Mrs Adams' wedding dress and put on my own clothes. It was so cold in the hallway I could almost see my breath. The cardboard and duct-tape window wasn't holding up. I walked past the living room and saw Abel and Carly asleep on the couch, lit up by the flashing TV on mute. Abel opened his eyes and saw me standing there. I waved at him with my fingers and he stood up, looking down at Carly to make sure she was still asleep. When he was sure, he silently walked with me to the front door and started to put on his boots.

When we got outside, it was snowing, and the wind whipped the snow off the ground into our faces. I hadn't worn a hat because I was having a good hair day. At least my hair was long and covered my ears. Abel wasn't wearing a hat either, but he had his curls. My jacket was pretty delusional too. I hated the down coats everyone wore. I wore a chic little pea coat. Fashion before comfort; you can be warm in hell.

Abel and I walked down the middle of the street because there was too much snow on the sidewalk. At the end of the block, a snowplow was stuck, beeping incessantly. We still didn't say anything. I didn't know what to say. I just wished he would put his arm around me because I was so cold. I remember thinking how if I were Carly, he would've put his arm around me.

We walked to the park without thinking, even though we were freezing and even though it was stupid to be outside. The snow was so deep, we sunk into it up to our knees. Abel swept the snow off the bench, and despite the fact that my teeth were chattering, I sat next to him. I didn't want to go home.

I waited, but nothing happened, so I finally took his arm and put it over my shoulder. I was worried that he might take it away, but he didn't. I think he wasn't worried about being seen; everyone else was either inside or frozen to death. It didn't make me feel the way I hoped it would. There wasn't anyone there to see, and that's what I really wanted.

I put my hand on his lap and started rubbing his jeans. I couldn't really feel it because my fingers were so numb. He looked around, but there was no one. He let me unzip his jeans, and pushed my head down on his lap as his head hung over the back of the bench. He tasted like a girl. My stomach swirled. My nose was running, and my mouth was dry.

He didn't even notice when I cried.

## *Fight Sequence*

My grandma came over to take me and Keefer to church the next Sunday morning. The irony that I prayed to a naked man in bondage was not lost on me. She came early so she could wash the dishes, which were always piled in the sink. "What your mother puts you boys through," she said, shaking her head and scraping dried spaghetti out of a pot.

I helped Keefer get ready because my grandma forced us to wear suits to church. They were hideous and matching; so uninspiring that I couldn't even trick my mind into believing I was at the Church of Scientology in Hollywood, where I went to be one with Xenu and Tom Cruise's dick.

My grandma got so involved in cleaning the house that she lost track of time. When Keef and I were dressed, I sat in the living room, staring at the clock, hoping she'd forget and we'd be so late she'd be too embarrassed to go.

When she saw the time on the stove, she started yelling loud enough that Ray moaned from the bedroom, the bedsprings creaking as he turned over. "We're late!" she gasped. "Why didn't you tell me what time it was?" She came flying into the living room in her Sunday best and yellow rubber gloves. She didn't stop shouting, "We're late!" until Ray threw a shoe at the door to shut her up. She was like a robo-nun gone haywire. Her rosary was steaming.

When we got in the car, my grandma sped out of the driveway and down the street. Every other time she drove she went ten miles an hour and prayed the entire time, but when she was late for church, the skin on our faces peeled back.

Keefer didn't mind church. He pretended to read the Bible upside down. At least he was more attentive than me; I just stared at Jesus, naked on the cross. He was the first man I ever had a crush on, even before Tobey Field. There was something about him—his face was so peaceful, even though he was in so much pain. He was the perfect submissive. If I had been Saint Veronica, I would have let him use my veil to wipe away his sweat and then sucked on it.

Keefer once asked me what heaven was, and I didn't know what to tell him, so I said it was "somewhere in the sky."

"Oh," he said, nodding. "But *what* is heaven?"

"How do I know?" I snapped, but he looked at me the way he would sometimes—like he thought I knew everything. "Well," I sighed, "I guess heaven is kind of like a fairy tale. You know how at the end of a fairy tale they say, 'and they lived happily ever after'?"

"Yeah."

"Well, I think maybe that's what heaven is. I think heaven is sort of like happily ever after."

But this is not a fairy tale.

When my grandma dropped me and Keefer off after church, my mom and Ray were fighting.

There's no place like home. There's no place like home. There's no place like home.

I went down to my room and put on the ruby slippers I'd stolen from the props department. I clicked my heels, hoping they'd work like reverse magic and take me away to Oz, my real home, where everyone is fabulous and freaky and sings catchy songs.

They didn't work. I could still hear the fighting which was so loud that Stoned Hairspray was hiding in the dryer. I took off the shoes and opened my door to go upstairs and get Keefer because I didn't want him hearing any more than he had to. But he was already sitting on the bottom step of the basement looking up at me.

"Are you hungry?" I asked, and his face lit up as he nodded.

We snuck out my window and went to the Day-n-Nite. Angela was there, sitting in our back booth. Keef and I went to sit with her, even though I wasn't sure if she wanted us to. She'd been ignoring my texts since I told her I was leaving town and was rarely at school. Angela always tried to hurt you before you could hurt her. She was very competitive about that kind of thing.

She didn't smile when Keef and I slid into the booth, but she didn't get up and leave either. A part of me regretted having told her. Maybe it would've been best if I had just left, if I was just another name under the booth of boys who had broken her heart.

I ordered Keefer fries and a shake, which I paid for with some of the money I'd saved. When he was done eating, he played with his action figures under the table.

"Shit," Angela said suddenly, ducking her head.

"What?" I asked. "I don't think there's enough room under there for the two of you, although you'd know better than me."

"Shut up," she whispered. "I just don't want to see them right now."

"Who?"

I turned around and saw Luke and Trey standing at the counter, both in sweats that showed their bulges and wearing baseball caps backward.

"What, don't want to see the future prom kings?"

"Not right now. And stop looking!"

"Trey is a nine, but Luke, Luke is an eleven. Although both of them together…"

"Oh God," Angela moaned. "Just shut up."

"That would be a twenty. Could you imagine?"

The parts of her cheek I could see turned red.

"Are you blushing?" I laughed. "Have I created a mental image that makes even the unconquerably provocative Angela Adams blush?"

"Fuck off. Are they still there?"

"I thought I wasn't supposed to look?"

"Just don't make it obvious."

I looked just as they turned to leave, the bells ringing on the door.

"They got it to go," I said.

Angela sat up and we watched them through the window as they got into Trey's truck.

"Now that I've gotten a good look from the back," I said, "I'm going to have to bump them each up a number."

"They are gorgeous, aren't they?" Angela sighed.

"I thought things were going well with you and Trey. Luke reeked like your perfume in English yesterday, so you must still be leaving your scent all over his house."

Angela didn't answer; she just stared through the glass after Luke and Trey.

"Let me guess, you've made your way through the team and found one you like better?" I laughed. "Oh, and did I tell you I'm seriously considering asking Luke to be my date to the Valentine's dance? If only to see the look on his face."

"Don't, dude."

"Why not?"

"Because that's retarded. It's never going to happen."

"A lot of people are afraid to say what they want," I said, "so they don't get it."

Angela just rolled her eyes as Keefer came up and started playing with his Transformer on the edge of the table. Brooke refilled our waters, and when she walked away, Keefer turned to me and asked, "She's a one, right, Jude?"

I turned to give Brooke a look-over behind the counter. "At first glance you might think so," I said, "since she does have varicose veins in her cankles, a pancake ass, and dollar-store nail polish. But when you take into account not only the mole on her chin but the hair sticking out of it, you come to the only logical conclusion: this is a rare case, meriting a rating in negative numbers. But, hey, God bless the ugly bitch. Every movie needs a character actor."

When Keefer and I got back from the Day-n-Nite, I was disappointed that there wasn't a *Cops* camera crew in my front yard.

My mom and Ray were still fighting. I lost track of how long it'd been. It was so bad, I couldn't even make it make-believe.

I went down to my room and stared at Luke's grade one picture, which I'd tucked under the frame of my mirror. He looked adorable—a kid with big blue eyes and blond hair. He was missing a tooth and was still tan from summer. I thought how, if we had kids, I'd like them to look just like him. But then I realized how stupid that was, so I tried not to think it. Sometimes, though, I couldn't help myself; I thought about stupid things, crazy stupid things that I knew would never actually happen, but which I thought about anyway because they filled me with hope—or delusion. But is that so bad? Sometimes you just have to keep fooling yourself or you'll never survive.

Keefer came downstairs crying. I wanted to tell him to cut it out—crying doesn't do anything but make you look like an even cheaper whore. But he was so helpless; I moved over so he could crawl into my bed with me and Stoned.

The fighting used to scare me too, but eventually, it became like TV background noise, always on way too loud, and the drama was so clichéd.

"Want to listen?" I asked Keefer, putting one of my earbuds in his ear.

"Why are Mom and Dad fighting?"

"Who knows," I shrugged, even though I heard her accuse him of stealing her tips to buy drugs. I almost had enough for a bus ticket. Soon I'd be on a Greyhound with no rear window, just a stinky toilet, so I couldn't look back even if I wanted to. Not that I would want to. No one looks back when they're going to heaven...And L.A. wasn't called the city of angels for nothing.

They got so loud that we could hear them over the music playing on my computer, and Keefer asked me if they were going to kill each other. I laughed, but I was kind of choked because he meant it. And the worst part was, I couldn't give him an answer.

"You bitch!" Ray screamed, followed by a shatter. I heard something smash against the wall, and I was scared it was my mom. "I'll fucking kill you!" Ray yelled, and my mom started screaming. But she wasn't screaming at him. She was just screaming.

"He's going to kill her," Keefer cried.

"Stay," I said, jumping out of bed. "Don't move."

I ran up to the living room. Ray had my mom pinned against the wall. His hands were wrapped around her neck and she was trying to push him away. When I think about it, it's like it happened to someone else. Everything was in fast forward. My head was spinning, and then I lost it.

I went for his hair. I pulled his head back so hard that his neck cracked. He spun around, sweat dripping from his eyebrows and down his stubble. Behind him, I saw my mom slide down the wall.

"Fucking faggot," he said, swinging his arm but stopping before he hit my face. I still sank to my knees, though, like it had been rehearsed.

He turned and walked out the door, slamming it so hard that what was left on the walls fell to the floor.

I looked across the room at my mom, who was surrounded by dirt and the broken pieces of a smashed flower pot. Keef's fish bowl was knocked over. In the middle of the living room floor, his goldfish was flopping on its side. He loved that thing. My mom saw it at the same time as me, and we both watched its last twitch. We couldn't save it; we couldn't do anything but watch it die.

My mom looked over at me, rubbing her neck. "What do we tell Keefer?" she asked.

I didn't answer her, but she didn't expect me to.

Eventually she got up and went to the bathroom, running herself a bath. I heard the cork pop on the wine bottle. When she started crying into her bubbles, I told myself to get up off the floor and tidy up—to hang the pictures back on the wall even if the frames were broken—but I couldn't move. I just stared at Keef's dead fish.

At least Keefer had listened to me and stayed down in the basement. I don't know if it was because he was obedient or afraid, but either way, it protected him. And he needed protecting from Ray. We all did.

One night, when I'd first moved down to the basement, I was having trouble sleeping. Everything was quiet except for occasional creaking floorboards. Ray was still up. My mom was at work. I got out of bed, hopping on dirty laundry to avoid the cold cement floor.

I climbed upstairs and peeked into Keefer's room. There were as many toys on his floor as there were clothes on mine. His eyes were closed, and his thumb was in his mouth, but when the hallway light streaked across his face, his eyes opened, and he pulled his hand away.

"Jude!" he smiled, but I could barely hear him over the hacking coming from the kitchen and that familiar smell.

"Goodnight," I said. "I just wanted to say goodnight. Stay in bed."

"Will you read to me?" he asked.

"No. Go to sleep. I'll see you tomorrow."

He was disappointed, but he nodded.

"Close your eyes," I told him, "and dream."

I walked silently to the kitchen. I knew what I was going to find, but I was still taken aback.

Ray was standing next to the sink in his dirty underwear. They had once been white but were now grey and torn at the elastic waist. He was skinnier than the last time I saw him naked—that time I walked in on him in the shower and he accused me of doing it on purpose.

He didn't see me as he dropped the pipe onto the kitchen floor. Smoke streamed out of his chapped lips and wrapped around his neck like a noose.

# 9021-Opiates

"Is it dead or alive?" Abel asked.

"Um..." I took a puff of the joint he passed me as we sat in the park. "I don't know. Did any whatsits decay?"

"It's dead and alive, dude," he said, laughing. He looked cute because his nose was so red and shiny and there were snowflakes in his cherubic curls.

"You cannot get me stoned and then start talking about this shit. My brain is imploding."

"It's quantum superposition."

"Could you imagine if your last name was Schrödinger? I guess you'd have to be a scientist. It's not like you could be a movie star."

"It's like, is that tree really there if we aren't looking at it?" he asked.

"Either you need to smoke less weed, or I need to smoke more."

"Just giving you some food for thought."

"Well, now I have the munchies."

"Day-n-Nite?"

"I can't. I'm saving. Did I tell you I almost have enough for a ticket?"

"Then what?"

"What do you mean?"

"Then what are you going to do? What's your plan once you actually get there?"

"I don't know," I shrugged. "Plans are for pussies."

"You can't just run away to Hollywood."

"Why not?"

"Because this isn't a movie."

"Says who?"

"People don't do things like that in real life."

"*This*," I sighed, "is not real."

"Have you told Angela?"

"Yeah. She's acting like I'm already gone."

"You know how she is. She doesn't want you to go."

"And neither do you," I smiled, poking his cheek with my frozen finger.

"I just don't think you realize what it's like out there," he said.

"And I don't think you realize what it's like here."

He thought about that for a while, looking at the frozen river.

"You're serious?" he asked, and I don't think I was imagining the sadness in his voice.

"I'm a big star, Abel. Just nobody knows it yet."

"But where are you going to live?"

"Oh, who cares where I live so long as I'm living?"

"Are you scared?"

"To go? No. But I'm scared to stay."

I waited for him to reach for my hand.

"What about you?" I asked. "Are you scared?"

"For you?"

"No, for yourself."

He shook some of the snow off his head.

"Not all of us can rock a busted nose quite like you, Jude."

I nodded, almost giving in and taking his hand, but I didn't have to. He reached for mine, and I was happy because I thought he never would.

"There's no stars tonight," he said.

I looked up at the black sky.

"So does that mean they don't exist?"

We didn't say much as we walked home, down the middle of the deserted street. I lit a cigarette, and he said, "I didn't know you smoked."

"Only when I want to feel like Bette Davis," I said.

His house was closest, so we stopped at the driveway. All the snow had been shovelled to the side. It was as high as the trash cans. I was going to walk the rest of the way home, but I didn't really want to go home, so I thought I might just keep walking.

"Well, goodnight," I said, but I didn't budge.

"If you're cold, you can come in and warm up," he offered, kicking ice with his foot. He wouldn't meet my eyes. "I mean, if you want."

"I am cold," I said, even though I wasn't. Sometimes you get so cold you stop feeling. He tried to hide his smile as I followed him to the front door. The censor light turned on like paparazzi hiding in the bushes. The spotlight could be so relentless.

We went to his room where he closed the door, keeping the lights off. I tried not to breathe because even that seemed too loud. When he whispered my name, I jumped and then couldn't stop giggling. He muffled my giggles with his tongue. He pulled off my shirt, and I unbuttoned his jeans, which were wet from sitting on the snowy park bench. Our breathing got heavier when we touched because our hands were so cold. He kissed me again, and when he pulled away I wondered if he was actually there if I couldn't see him. We tripped over our clothes on the floor and landed on the bed. He pulled the covers over our heads and everything became even darker. If my asshole hadn't been brimming with his spit, I wouldn't have believed it.

It didn't hurt as much as Angela said it would. When I wanted to gasp, moan, scream, he covered my mouth with his hand, so it echoed in my head. His breathing got heavier and then he trembled, and it was over. I felt him go soft inside of me as I held onto him. We were stuck together with sweat. His whole body shook. He cried without making a sound, but I felt a tear roll off his cheek and land on my face. He passed out in my arms. I don't know how long we stayed like that with my hands tangled in his knotted hair like I was trying to pray. I couldn't tell if I was sleeping; it was so dark, I thought my eyes were closed even when they were open.

When I woke up there was some light coming through the window, but the sky was mostly cloudy. The bed had shifted so there was a space between it and the wall, which half of Abel's body was falling into.

I got out of bed quietly, trying not to wake him. I knew it would be awkward. I wanted to touch his hair but didn't let myself. I kept thinking how he was sort of like Schrödinger's cat. He was gay *and* straight, depending on how you looked at it. I didn't really know if the cat was dead or alive, or if Abel was gay or straight. But I thought either way, it must be so terrible for both of them, trapped in that box.

I couldn't find my shirt, and I wanted to get out of there, so I picked up one of Abel's from the floor. It was wrinkled, had a grease stain near the collar, and it smelled like his sweat. I was never going to give it back.

I forgot to listen at the door before I opened it, and ran into Mrs Adams coming out of the bathroom. She was wearing a pink housecoat and her peroxide hair was dishevelled, her roots a mix of brown and grey.

"Oh, good morning, Jude," she yawned, rubbing her eyes as I closed Abel's door. "Did you and Angela have a nice sleep-over?"

"Yes," I nodded.

"Abel has a shirt just like that," she said, giving me a lopsided smile.

"Weird," I shrugged, walking down the hall. "Well, have a nice day, Mrs Adams."

"Yes, it is getting late isn't it?" she said, stumbling back to her room.

I let myself out the front door, grateful for, and craving, Mrs Adams' private pharmacy.

I listened to music off my phone, dancing by myself down the middle of the dead street because the sidewalks still needed to be shovelled. When I was a block from my house, I saw his truck and froze, almost dropping my phone.

Soap stars never die.

# *Typecast*

The last time I'd seen him was during the summer. Only I didn't really see him. I was in the hospital, and it was the middle of the night, but I was awake. I didn't want to fall asleep; when I closed my eyes, the snuff films played.

I still hadn't looked in the mirror. I could tell by the way Keefer looked at me when he came to visit that I didn't want to. He brought me a card he made in art class with a big red heart on the front, and he hadn't learned how to draw in the lines yet. Or maybe he had and just didn't give a shit.

I heard footsteps coming into the room and closed my eyes. Whoever it was walked in and stopped, then took a few more steps and pulled back the curtain. At first I thought it was a doctor, and I was glad that my eyes were closed. But then I smelled stale cigarette smoke.

I could feel my dad watching me, and my heart sped up—I knew it was him. I felt his breath as he leaned over, as he touched my bandaged forehead. I told myself to open my eyes, but I couldn't; I didn't think that he'd understand.

"I love you, kid," he said.

Then I heard shoes clicking on the linoleum floor down the hallway. I sensed him stand up and back away from me as the footsteps got closer until they reached the room. I heard a nurse say, "Sir, what are you doing in here?" He mumbled something, but I couldn't make it out. "It's way past visiting hours," she said, and he muttered some more. I heard him walk past her, out of the room.

I kept telling myself to open my eyes and stop him before he was gone, but it was like my lids were stuck together, like that time I used too much of my mom's eyelash glue. Then it was too late: he and the nurse had left my room, their voices waning.

When everything was silent again, I thought I might have imagined it. I kept sniffing, but there was no trace of cigarette smoke.

It really haunted me, lying there, thinking about how that was the first time my dad had ever told me that he loved me, and I might've made it up.

I stood on the street and watched as my dad came out of the house. Mom stood in the doorway. He was wearing a baseball cap, which shaded his eyes. Sometimes, my parents would stop being Elizabeth Taylor and Richard Burton in *Who's Afraid of Virginia Woolf?* and be civil to each other. It always freaked me out. He slowly walked toward me, and I held my breath.

"How's it going, kid?" he asked, and I think I shrugged before he asked if I wanted to get some breakfast. I must've nodded and walked to his truck and put on my seat belt and maybe even listened to the radio as he drove us to the Day-n-Nite. That's where we ended up. It was like I blinked my eyes and we were sitting at a front booth. I didn't realize I was there until I looked up and saw Brooke flirtatiously pouring his coffee.

I excused myself and went to the bathroom where I leaned against the sink, looking at myself in the mirror. I had dark circles under my eyes and messy hair. My bottom lip was chapped, and it looked like the grease stain on Abel's shirt had gotten even bigger. I don't know how that happened—probably just from walking through the air in the Day-n-Nite. My hands were shaking so hard that I thought I might pull the sink from the wall.

I went into a stall that was darker than the rest of the bathroom because the light above it was busted. It was too dark to see, but it smelled like I was standing in a puddle of piss. I leaned over and puked.

When I came out of the bathroom, Brooke was standing at our table, refilling my dad's coffee. She asked me if I wanted any, and I nodded.

"Gonna stunt your growth," my dad said as Brooke walked away, her big feet squeaking in a pair of clogs. But then he looked out the window like he knew it was a lame thing to say. As he looked away, I picked up a butter knife and held it under the table. I glanced at him. He looked about the same as the last time we shot a scene together. Maybe a little more dried up.

"You hungry?" he asked, his voice gruff.

"Sure," I shrugged. He looked out the window again, and I pressed the butter knife harder against my wrist.

"So," he turned back to me, "where'd you sleep?"

"I had a night shoot," I said.

He spun his coffee cup on the table top. I looked down at my arm. I'd broken the scab on a cut, and there was a bit of blood trickling down my wrist. Brooke came back, and my dad ordered toast and, even though I was starving, I ordered the same because I wanted to get breakfast over with.

"I thought you were hungry," he said, like he was offended.

"I think I'm just tired."

"The coffee tastes like dirt in this place," he sighed. "I had a rough night, too, driving," he said, sipping his dirt. "I've been driving for sixteen hours." He paused like he was waiting for me to ask him from where, but I didn't want to know. Just another place on the map. He tapped his fingers on the table. His nails were short and jagged like mine. We had the same hands. I always thought of him when I looked at my hands. Especially when they were around my dick. He always popped into my mind at the more absurd moments. My hands were the only manly thing about me. I'd put on one of my mom's dresses and almost get away with it, except for the hands; they always gave me away. They were never elegant, no matter what colour I painted my nails.

"Why is it every time I see you, you're even more roughed up?" he asked.

"I don't have a portrait in my attic," I shrugged.

"What?"

"Nothing," I sighed, looking back out the window.

"Your scar's not so bad," he smiled. "Makes you look tough."

I didn't say anything, and he took another sip of his coffee. I waited for him to slurp like Ray, but then remembered that my dad never slurped. He swatted me across the head when I was little because I was grating my teeth against my fork. He was crazy about table etiquette. I used to resent him for it, but I figured it would come in handy when I was in Hollywood, going to dinner parties in Beverly Hills with socialites and trust-fund hipsters.

"Your mom says she kicked him out," my dad said.

I felt the blood dripping down the side of my wrist. "Like that'll last."

"Yeah," he nodded, tapping his fingers even harder. "I wanted to give you something," he said, reaching into his pocket as Brooke brought us our toast and packets of jam. Once she was gone, he put an envelope in front of my plate.

"Open it," he said.

It was a cheque. It wasn't a fortune, but it was more than I had ever seen from him and enough to get me to Los Angeles in the back of a limousine. Arrivals are everything.

"What is this for?" I asked.

"I missed a few birthdays," he said, silently biting into his toast. Not a single crumb fell onto the plate in front of him.

"You missed all of them. How did you get it?"

"It doesn't matter how I got it. I got it for you."

"Stolen car parts?"

"Don't be a little shit," he said, lowering his eyes and looking offended.

"You don't have to buy me," I told him.

"Good. Don't be like your mother, only feeling beautiful when she's being bought."

"Well, I hope you don't expect me to put this into a college fund or something."

"No, you're probably going to beauty school, right?" He looked right at me and didn't say it exactly mockingly, but I still felt like I should be ashamed.

"A cosmetologist? As if," I said. "I'm most stereotypes, but not that one. Do I look like the help?"

"No," he sighed. "Just like you need it." He looked down at his plate, and I couldn't tell if he was being serious, but it didn't matter; he was already starting to space out. "Use the money for whatever you want," he said. "Just don't blow it. Or blow it if you want. It's yours."

I looked at him, and he took a bite of his toast, and I didn't know what to say.

"Thank you," I finally said, folding the cheque and slipping it in my pocket. The action line in the screenplay told me to smile, but I ignored it.

We finished our toast and then got back in his truck. His visits were always ephemeral; he didn't get much screen time because he was terrible at remembering his lines and always missed his cue. He would hold up production, or stop it all together.

The radio played as we drove, but we didn't say much. He lit a cigarette and unrolled the window as I relaxed in my seat with blood dripping down my arm. I just kept thinking about how the truck drivers in the Day-n-Nite hadn't checked me out once. I felt so ugly when I wasn't being desired.

My dad pulled up to the driveway of the house, and before I got out I said, "See you soon," which felt like such a stupid thing to say. Fire the screenwriter! He took a drag of his cigarette and rested his elbow on the window.

"See ya later," he nodded.

I didn't watch him drive away.

My mom and Keefer were sitting at the kitchen table when I walked in the house. Keefer was eating a PB&J, and my mom was circling listings in the newspaper with nail polish in "I'm Not Really A Waitress" red.

"Job hunting," my mom said as I sat down at the table. "I don't want to be like Ginger Rogers, dancing beyond my prime."

"All you want is to be Ginger Rogers, Mom. But it's okay. Who doesn't?"

"Who's Ginger Rogers?" Keefer asked.

"I didn't expect you to be home so soon," my mom said. "Is he gone?"

"I guess."

"He didn't say?"

"Who's Ginger Rogers?" Keefer screamed.

"A dancer," I said.

"A dancer?" He stuck out his tongue, which was covered with peanut butter. "I don't want to be a stupid dancer."

"No one said you had to be."

"You didn't ask him?" my mom asked, touching up her nails now.

"Did too! You said everyone wants to be Ginger Rogers."

"He's gone, Mom," I said. "What else is there?"

The next morning, I went to the bank. The cheque didn't bounce. I stared at the balance until the numbers blurred. My fingers were so damp that they made the deposit slip transparent. I thought about putting my mom's tips back on her dresser, but I figured I needed them. My dad's money would barely cover my first Hollywood overdose. I didn't feel guilty about taking my mom's tips; I guess I thought she'd probably want me to have them, once I was really there and she knew I wasn't coming back.

I wanted to tell her I was going, but couldn't. She'd never let me go, and I had no choice. I felt like I was being summoned. Like my whole life had been leading up to this point. Like I had to deal with so much hate just to make my skin thick enough so that the spotlight wouldn't burn.

I walked from the bank to the bus station and bought the ticket. The night bus out of town on Friday, February 12. I'd leave right after the Valentine's dance. My A-list farewell party.

When I got home, I put the ticket in the shoe box filled with singles under my bed, checking every couple minutes to make sure it was still there. I sat on the edge of my bed listening to Bronski Beat's "Smalltown Boy" on repeat. Even leaving town was a cliché, but I didn't care. I had been typecast in utero, and I was going to get an Oscar if it cost me my life.

I was too excited to sleep, so I went for a walk at night and ended up on the side of the highway. I hadn't realized how far I had gone until I looked up and saw the Welcome sign. It was chipped, and the wood was rotting. One look at it and you'd slam on your brakes and turn right around.

It said "Welcome to hell." Someone had crossed out the name of our town and spray-painted "hell" in red letters over it. I laughed, imagining my grandma's expression when she saw it.

It was snowing, and I could hardly see. It was like the air was white. But I could see the letters on the sign, dripping like blood. The snow was so deep it was pulling me under, seeping into my boots. I looked down the highway. It was a long black stroke of ink that told a never-ending story. I stood and I waited, and every time I saw a pair of headlights through the storm, I was sure it was him.

# *Hidden Feature*

"**L**isa's gone vegan," Mr Dawson said. "Care for a pita and hummus?"

"Sure," I shrugged, taking his brown paper lunch bag. "What are you going to eat?"

"I'll run down to the cafeteria once the line dies down."

"Why does she want you to be vegan?"

"Because she think it'll make me—" He stopped and smiled. "Because she thinks it'll help us conceive."

"Really?"

"She read that vegan men have stronger sperm."

"A baby?"

"Yes," he laughed, "a baby."

"But think about how horrible it'll be to wake up every morning and think about someone else before you think about yourself."

"You don't think that would be liberating?"

"Because then who's thinking of you?"

"I think it'll be a nice reprieve."

"But if no one is thinking about you, then do you exist?"

"What?"

"It's like, the cat is dead and alive, but if you never think about it, it's like it was never even there."

"Has Mr Hurst been drinking before physics again?" he laughed.

"Hey, guess what?" I asked. "I'm ready to move to Hollywood and sell my soul to the devil! Will you miss me?"

"Still on Hollywood, huh? Fame is your generation's AIDS." He leaned back in his chair and started playing with his tie. "But I'm glad you have a dream, Jude. I just wish you'd leave the devil out of it."

"Not possible," I said. "Just ask the Kar*trash*ians."

"Well, only a few more years and you'll be free to move to L.A., where you can ask Kris Jenner for tips on how not to smudge while writing in blood on the dotted line."

"Ah, reality-show contracts," I sighed. "But I'm not waiting. I'm way too interesting to wait."

"So what's the plan then, you hitchhiking on out of here?"

"No, I don't want to get killed before I get there—my stalker would be so disappointed. I bought a bus ticket."

"Really?" Mr Dawson asked. "When are you going?"

I was about to tell him everything; how they were rolling out the red carpet for me as we spoke. But I didn't because, suddenly, I knew he'd try to stop me. He'd call my mom. He'd tell himself he was doing it because it was the right thing to do, but really, it'd be because he didn't want to see me go. "Just for a couple days," I said quickly. "I'm going to see my dad."

"You've never mentioned your dad before," he said, like he already didn't believe me. "Where are you staying?"

"The Chateau Marmont, of course."

"Really?"

"Yeah," I nodded, even though I knew I had gone off script.

"With your dad?" he asked, and we were just improvising now.

"Yeah, he's a movie star. A really famous one."

Mr Dawson didn't say anything, didn't even blink.

"He was filming a movie around here, that's how he met my mom," I said, and I could see it. I could believe it. My Hollywood father with wavy blond hair and chestnut eyes. "He had to keep me out of the tabloids because he had a wife at the time. America's sweetheart, you know—the whole deal. She was in the movies too. So I never really got to see him much. But this is going to make up for it."

"Sounds like a dream," he said.

"Yeah," I smiled, believing it, really believing it. I looked out of the window. It felt like it had been snowing forever. "So what are you and Lisa doing for Valentine's Day?" I asked.

"Not much, I'm afraid. We'll have to try and squeeze something in. She has to work on the weekend, and I'm chaperoning the dance on Friday. The school was short on volunteers."

"I'll save you a dance," I said, and he chuckled as he stood up, grabbing his wallet off his desk.

"I'm going to run down to the caf," he said. "Hopefully the hormone-raging freaks will be eating their hormones, not waiting in line for them."

"Are you going to get the chubby cancer burger?"

"No," he shook his head from the doorway. "I think I'm in the mood for a ham and disease."

He left the classroom, and I was sitting alone when I saw Angela and Luke walk past the door. They didn't notice me, but I almost fell out of my desk because I hadn't seen Angela since we were at the Day-n-Nite with Keef. I called and texted her, but got no reply. She'd been skipping the classes we had together.

I understood why she was ignoring me. It was easier. I thought maybe I should just let her push me away, but I couldn't. I loved her too much. So I stuck my head out the door and was about to call her name before she turned down the stairwell. But someone pressed pause, and I remembered what she'd told me.

"I would never do that to you," she'd said.

I followed them. I ran to my locker, got my coat, and stepped in their footprints as they cut through the field to Luke's house. They didn't turn around once. I almost wanted them to because then I could stop following them. I'd already know, I'd see it all over their faces.

When they reached his house, I stayed back and watched them go through the front door. I waited behind a tree and then walked up the front steps. An icicle hung from the roof and dripped onto my head. I looked through the window but couldn't see anyone inside. Breaking and entering isn't as glamorous as a DUI, but I thought maybe I'd start a new trend. I took a deep breath and opened the door, stepping inside. They were already upstairs.

The house looked different without people partying in it. It felt warm, and not just because I was coming from outside; it smelled like leftovers, like meat and potatoes. The carpet needed to be vacuumed. There was taxidermy mounted on the walls. The fridge was covered with pictures and magnets. A schnauzer stood up from its mat near the back door, and I was worried it was going to bark, but it just wagged its stumpy tail.

Hearing them together upstairs wasn't enough. Maybe I was a masochist; I wanted to know without a shred of doubt. I'd hold onto the pieces and keep trying to put them together.

Careful not to make any noise, I slowly climbed the stairs. I didn't have to go all the way up. I could see them through the banister. Luke's bedroom door was open, and they were on the unmade bed. His hand ran up her back and undid the snap of her bra. Angela's nipples were pierced. He grabbed one with his hand and put it in his mouth. Her head fell back, her eyes closed, and her mouth opened. If she moaned, I didn't hear.

I ran back down the stairs and out the door, leaving it open behind me. I could hear the dog barking all the way down the block.

I didn't drop to my knees, gasping for breath, until the director called "Cut!" and everything faded to black.

# *Rewrite*

When I got home, I found all the pictures of Angela I had, including the pictures she had taken of me, and started burning them with my lighter, letting them turn to ash on the basement floor. I thought watching her burn would be satisfying, but it just made me sad. I couldn't hate Angela. If it hadn't been for our friendship, I wouldn't have had anyone to write my suicide letters to.

When my head healed from Matt's skateboard attack and I got out of the hospital, I don't think I would've been able to show myself at school if I hadn't known Angela would be by my side.

Before the first day back, I put a ton of makeup over my scar, trying to make it disappear. No matter how much vitamin E I had rubbed on it, it was still purple. I thought about giving myself bangs, but decided I'd rather be teased about the scar.

My mom was home from work and still awake. She was standing in the kitchen smoking a cigarette when I came upstairs.

She asked if I wanted breakfast and pointed to a box of cereal on the table. I could hear Keef watching cartoons in the living room. I told her I wasn't hungry. She nodded and offered to drive me to school. I told her I wanted to walk and she didn't say anything, but I knew what she was thinking. The cigarette between her fingers burned, the ash grew long. She hugged me before I left, but I didn't hug her back. My whole body stiffened. I didn't look at her because she was crying, and I was embarrassed that she'd stayed awake for me.

I met Angela outside the Day-n-Nite. She was sitting on the sidewalk, making more rips in her tights with a razor that had dried blood on it.

"Nervous?" she asked.

I shook my head but could tell she didn't believe me.

We smoked a joint as we walked the rest of the way to school, but it just made me paranoid. Angela was chill. Her head was back and she smiled with her eyes half-closed behind her orange-tinted glasses.

Nothing out of the ordinary happened in the morning. People stared and talked about me, but I was used to it. I told myself I was Lilo. People always stared and talked about me. When I was in line for a juice in the caf, the girls behind me talked about me like I wasn't standing right in front of them.

"I thought he killed himself?" they said, sounding disappointed.

Colin cut up his eraser into tiny pieces and threw them at me all through math whenever Mrs Kennedy turned her back. I sat so still I wasn't sure I was alive. A piece of eraser whipped my ear and it stung, but I didn't react.

I loved my haters.

At lunch, a big crowd hung around the bleachers. They all turned and stared as I walked by with Angela, who was smoking a cigarette. Luke looked down so that he didn't have to look at me, and Matt yelled, "Whoever helped you to the hospital should be shot!"

I stopped and turned around. Angela said, "Fuck him, Jude," and rolled her eyes.

"You should've been left to die," Matt said, shaking his head and laughing.

"Eat shit," Angela snapped, flipping him off.

I waited for Luke to look at me, but he didn't.

"Say goodbye to your friend," Matt taunted Angela, making his hand into a gun and pointing it in my direction.

Angela would have jumped onto the bleachers and strangled Matt if I had let her. That's why reducing her to ashes didn't appease my rage. I gave up on her, taking Luke's grade school photo off my mirror instead.

I flicked the lighter in my hand, on and off, losing myself somewhere between light and darkness.

I kissed the picture, then held the flame to the edge and watched it burn.

I wanted to kiss it again, once he was gone. But it was too late.

He was already ashes.

I fell asleep on the cutting room floor and woke up with fragments of Luke and Angela stuck to my cheek.

It was the last day of filming. The school Valentine's dance was to be the wrap party. After that I'd be on a bus, playing a new character.

I went to school just because I thought I might go crazy with anticipation if I stayed home all day. And I was curious if Angela would show up—if I'd get to see her. I knew she had to do it, she had to get me back. If I hadn't caught them, I don't think she would've told me. She didn't do it to hurt me. She did it to even things out so that she could sleep at night, knowing she wasn't the only one who'd been betrayed. I was leaving, and I thought I might never see her again, but it didn't make me sad. I stopped feeling anything real after I saw her with Luke. It was easy to make believe when everyone was so fake.

There was no point in class that day; everyone was too hyped up on cinnamon hearts or Oxy. All the pretty girls gave each other roses. Even the lipstick on Mrs Kennedy's teeth was red.

Luke was at school, standing at the end of the hallway with Matt and all their friends, his arm around Madison.

I don't know how I ended up in front of them. They looked up at me, and if the camera had flashed for the photo, they would've had red eyes.

Madison raised her eyebrow and waited. The director had called, "Quiet on set, camera rolling!"

"Luke," I said, swallowing the vomit caught in my throat. It went back down and made my eyes water. He looked at me and his face went hard. I could tell he was terrified. "Luke," I said again, even though he was already listening. Everyone was.

"What?" he asked, deadpan.

"Will you be my Valentine?"

Matt started laughing, and Madison said, "Oh my God, you're joking, right?"

"You know you love me," I said, my dying words.

"You're a faggot," Luke sneered, already looking away. If he wasn't looking at me, was I there?

"Yeah? Well, so are you. Why don't you just admit it already?"

"What did you just say?" Madison laughed.

"What, didn't you tell them, Luke?"

"Tell us what?" Matt asked.

"About how he came back."

"Shut up," Luke said, looking at me again. I was alive!

"He came back. Luke saved me that night. It was him."

"You're fucking kidding me," Matt said, turning to Luke for confirmation and finding it in his pupils, which dilated with fear, or maybe with regret for having a conscience. It's the only thing that can make your star fade.

"He was my hero," I cried, and I knew this was the reel I'd send in for awards.

"Shut up," Luke said through gritted teeth. He was so close.

"Don't be shy, Luke. We love each other. That's why you saved me. Because you love me. And that's why every time you came to visit me at the hospital, I gave you the best—"

"Shut the fuck up!" He screamed, lunging at me.

I didn't step back. I took a breath, trying to take him in. I wanted to feel it. But he stopped himself. He came so close to me that I could've kissed him, but then Matt yelled, so the whole hallway could hear, "Luke Morris is a faggot!" And even though I could've puckered my lips, I was too busy watching his quiver.

The bell rang, and Mr Dawson appeared at his classroom door, ushering us in. Matt was smiling wider than his future beer belly.

Mr Dawson started class by reading aloud, but no one was paying attention. No one even knew what he was reading. Everyone was tweeting under their desks. Matt was already trying to trend "#LuJu."

Then Matt looked up from his phone, right at Luke, and started simulating a blow job, poking his tongue in his cheek. Madison made a show of sliding her desk as far away from Luke's as possible. Mr Dawson stopped reading and glared at her when the desk squeaked against the floor. A few people burst out laughing as Matt exaggerated a gag. Mr Dawson looked like he was ready to throw the book at them, but he didn't have a chance. Luke stood up, pushed over his desk, and stormed out of class. Madison screamed when the desk flipped and crashed to the floor, but you could tell she wasn't scared, it was like she had planned it. Like she had fucked for the part and been cast for the way she screamed.

I watched Luke go, wishing that I could run after him. I wanted to tell him that I was sorry, that I was stupid, that I didn't mean it. I just couldn't help myself. I knew he wasn't going to say "yes" to being my Valentine, but I'd had to ask, even if it wasn't in the script.

I said my lines anyway, hoping there'd been a rewrite.

As soon as class ended, I went to the bathroom to look for him. I don't know what I would've said if I had found him. I don't know whether I would've apologized or rubbed it in. I wanted him to love me, but if he wouldn't, I wanted him to hate me because love and hate are two sides of the same coin, and I wanted Luke to spend everything on me.

When I walked through the bathroom door, Kenny and Colin were standing at the urinals, and Matt was fixing his hair at the mirror.

"What are you doing in the boys' room, Judy?" Matt asked.

I should've turned around and left, but I had too much pride. Even though I didn't have to go, I walked past him into a stall that looked like it hadn't been flushed for a week. I gagged and tried to breathe through my mouth.

"What, is Luke in there with you?" Matt laughed, pulling the door open.

I went over to the sink, trying not to throw up. The whole bathroom stunk like shit.

"Don't forget to wash," Matt said.

I turned on the tap and put my hands under the water. I wasn't thinking. I should've just ran.

"Your face," Matt said. "Don't forget to wash your face."

Kenny and Colin came up on each side of me before I had the chance to get away. But the worst part was, even if I'd had a chance, I don't know if I would have run away. Sometimes I became a freeze frame.

I resisted at first, but Kenny twisted my wrist so hard it cracked. There was no point in fighting them. Matt held open the door of the stall I had just been in, and they dragged me toward the clogged toilet.

"Fucking righteous, man," Kenny laughed. "I think this is the stall I used this morning." He took a big sniff. "Yep, that's my Taco Time all right."

They forced me to my knees. I would've screamed, but I was scared of opening my mouth. I started to struggle out of sheer desperation, but Kenny grabbed the back of my head so hard I thought he was going to rip out my hair.

"Just pretend the water is Luke's cock," Matt said, right before my face broke the filthy surface, "and blow."

They held me under, then lifted me back up so I could take a breath before holding me under again. I zoned out. We were in a prison shower, they were three Aryan skinheads gang-raping me. I felt so needed. They liked to take turns putting on my makeup and then smudging it. One of the crew members kept giving me pain killers. Every time I moaned, the camera picked up the glitter pills I was gargling.

Once they got bored, they let me fall to the floor, spitting shit.

"I thought for sure you swallowed," Matt said, kicking me in the gut.

They walked out, laughing. I crawled over to the sink, using it to help me stand. I looked in the mirror. My face was pale where it wasn't bruised, and dirty water dripped from my hair. I leaned over the sink and puked, then held my head under the tap to wash away the shit.

When I looked back up at my reflection, everything was blurred. I batted my eyes and tried to give my best face, my red carpet face, but it was so faded, I looked like a grainy paparazzi shot. I punched the mirror, and the glass cracked, falling to my feet like lost scenes.

Everyone stared at me as I walked down the hall. My skin was cocaine white, which made the blood dripping to my feet look even more red. I had been cast in a horror movie and just come back from the dead. "Jude," Mr Dawson said when he smelled me at the door. "What in hell?" He rushed over and almost touched my filthy, wet hair but stopped himself.

"And your hand!" he gasped as blood dripped onto his loafers. He took my arm and led me to his desk. "We have to get this cleaned up." He sat me in his chair and took a handful of tissue to wipe up the blood. "I think you might need stitches," he said. "What happened?"

I tried to speak, but it was like the bathroom mirror had broken in my throat.

"Shit," Mr Dawson said, "this isn't going to cut it." He dropped the tissue into the waste basket next to his desk and grabbed the scarf hanging with his coat on a hook behind me.

"This'll have to do for now, but let's get you to the nurse's office. Who did this?" he demanded, wrapping my hand.

"I don't want to be here anymore," I murmured.

Mr Dawson took it the wrong way and hugged me, like he was scared I was going to try and break through the classroom window.

"Don't say that," he said. "Please don't say that. You have no idea how incredible you are." He started crying, and I was impressed; most of my co-stars needed Visine. "You have no idea how brilliant you are. How brilliant your life is going to be." My lips were trembling, so he put a finger on them. "There's nothing to be afraid of," he said.

Then he removed his finger from my lips and kissed them.

# *Hollywood Ending*

My feet didn't touch the ground as I ran out of Mr Dawson's classroom, down the hall, and out of the door. I ran until I found myself standing in front of Keefer's school. I sat on the bench outside the gate. It was recess, and all the kids were playing in the field. I spotted Keef right away because he was wearing his long dragon hat. He was throwing snowballs with some other kids.

As he ran, the tail of the dragon hat trailed behind him, and some kid pulled it off his head. I watched Keef chase him around the entire schoolyard, but he couldn't catch him. I looked at the teacher, waiting for her to do something, but she was on her phone. Keefer kept chasing him, but the kid was too fast. I wanted to climb onto the field and rip the hat out of his hand, but before I could, the kid ran up to the gate and threw it over. It landed on a snowbank right next to me. Keefer came to the gate, sticking his fingers through, and I stood up to get it for him. His face was red, but I couldn't tell if it was from the cold. He hated it when I came to his school.

"What are you doing here?" he asked me as I tossed the hat to him with my good hand. The kid who took it stood a couple feet away with a group of boys.

"I don't know," I shrugged.

"You're all wet."

"I was making snow angels."

"Why aren't you in school?"

"I don't have school today."

"Liar."

"What do you know?" I smiled.

"Where's your jacket?" he asked. "Aren't you cold?"

"No," I shook my head. "I don't feel anything."

"You look funny. Why do you have a scarf around your hand?"

"Stop with the questions!"

"Your lips are blue," he said.

"It's lipstick."

"No it isn't. Your lipstick is pink."

"You're right," I laughed.

"What are you doing here?" he asked again.

The bell rang, and most of the kids headed for the school, but Keefer stayed, aware of the boys still standing behind him.

"Hey, Keefer," the kid who'd taken his hat yelled, "is that your brother or your sister?"

"Why did you come here?" Keefer asked me, pulling his dragon hat over his ears.

"I just wanted to say goodbye," I said, but he was already running inside.

I stood there even after he was gone, looking at the snowy field stamped with footprints. As I started to walk home, I thought about when Keefer and I still shared a room. One time, when he played on his bed, I sat in front of the mirror, putting on makeup. Madonna played on my iTunes, and I sang along. Keefer kept looking up from his Lego, watching me paint my face.

Our mom was at work, and Ray had been missing for a few days. Keefer had stopped asking where he was. I don't know if he didn't ask because he didn't want to upset Mom or if he had just stopped caring, but I thought it was probably both.

Through the corner of my eye I saw him drop his Lego and sigh. I swear, sometimes the kid was more dramatic than me. "What's the beef, Keef?" I asked.

"I'm bored."

"Only boring people are bored."

He rolled off the bed and came up to me, picking up a brush and bending the bristles. "Why do you dress up like a girl?"

I kept my eyelashes in the curler as I said, "You know on Halloween when you get to dress up?"

He nodded.

"It makes you happy, right?"

"Yeah."

"Well, dressing up makes me happy, too. But I just don't want to wait for Halloween."

He thought about it for a second and then said, "Okay," with a little shrug of his shoulders. "Are you going out tonight?"

"Sure am."

"Where?"

"Somewhere over the rainbow."

"I want to come."

"You're too boring."

"Am not."

"Prove it," I said, opening a tube of lipstick. He hesitated for a second then laughed and took it from my hands, smearing it all over his mouth. "Don't break it," I said, taking the tube from him and carefully applying some to his lips.

"More!" he yelled, like it was a game, like every day is Halloween.

I did his eyes and then taught him how to pout.

"I look like a girl," he said. "I look like you."

I started lip syncing to "Hollywood," and Keefer danced. We didn't hear the front door open or the sound of his dirty boots as he came down the hallway. I took a tissue and told Keefer to blot, but he didn't know what blotting was, so he told me he didn't have any snot. I laughed, throwing my head back, and that's when I saw Ray's eyes at the top of the mirror.

"What are you doing?" he asked, and his voice gave me chills. Keefer spun around and faced him.

"Daddy!" Keef laughed. "Jude made me pretty!"

It happened so fast. Ray grabbed Keefer's arm and dragged him out of the room. Keef started crying down the hallway, and I tried to stand, I swear I did, but my knees were weak. I sank to the floor. I heard a slap. Ray yelled, "What do you think you are, a little faggot?" I tried to get off the floor, tried to drag myself to the door, but I was stuck. "Are you a little faggot?" Ray was yelling. I couldn't move. I heard the shower turn on, and Keefer's cries turned to screams.

"It's hot," he screamed. "Daddy, it's hot!" I couldn't move. I lay there and cried and couldn't move. I couldn't save him. I wanted to. But I couldn't.

I couldn't even save myself.

By the time I got home from Keefer's school, the blood on my hand had dried, and the scarf was practically fused to it.

I expected my mom to still be sleeping, but she was awake and in the kitchen, cooking, with her hair in rollers. She was wearing her bra and panties, an apron, and nothing else except the fake pearls I gave her for Christmas. Her dress was on the ironing board. She had a cigarette dangling between her lips, and the ash looked dangerously close to falling into whatever it was that she was burning. My mom always looked poetically trailer trash.

"You're home early," she said, taking the cigarette out of her mouth and crunching it into the crystal ashtray next to the sink.

"We had early dismissal because of the dance tonight," I lied, hiding my hand behind my back.

"You must be excited!" she said, but she didn't even look over at me. "I have to work on Sunday, you know. It's a big night for the club, so I'm cooking a dinner tonight for me and—" She stopped herself before she said his name.

"What are you and Ray having?" I asked. I was trying to make it easier for her, but I couldn't hide the contempt in my voice.

She had her back turned, but as she closed the oven door, I bet she closed her eyes too.

"Roast beef," she said, leaning on the stove. "Don't look at me like that!" she said, even though her back was still to me. She reached for her pack of cigarettes on the counter and lit another one. "He's sorry," she exhaled, turning to face me but not registering the way the makeup artist had made me grotesque. Maybe the cigarette smoke was too thick.

"I know that doesn't mean much because he's said it so many times before, but what do you want me to do?"

I didn't say anything.

"Damn it, Jude. What do you want me to do? He's a bastard, but he's my bastard. You don't want me to end up alone, do you? I'm too old to go looking for a new boyfriend." She took a long drag. "I need him. No one is hiring after Christmas, anyway," she said. "I should really wait until spring to find a job."

I nodded.

"He's sorry," she pleaded. "He's going to tell you so himself. He feels bad about everything. You know how he is."

"It's okay, Mom."

"No, it isn't okay. But at least he didn't hit you."

"What about you?"

"He knows he isn't welcome back in this house unless he changes." Her eyes were so desperate, I couldn't take it. She took a drag of her cigarette, and half of it was gone.

"Okay," I said.

"Are you all right?" she asked, waving away the smoke. "Are you sick? You look sick."

"I'm fine," I said, walking toward the bathroom. "Just cold."

I took a long shower and then went down to my room to bandage my hand. It wasn't that bad. It's not like I could see bone or anything. I covered most of the cuts and tried not to move my fingers too much because every time they bent, my knuckles bled.

Then I packed my suitcase with my favourite clothes, shoes, and makeup. I put the holy trinity, *People, Star,* and *In Touch,* in my backpack. I also had Candy Darling's *My Face for the World to See* to read as inspiration on the bus. Candy was like me. Stubble showed through her powder, and too much of everything was never enough.

Stoned Hairspray curled up in my suitcase. I think she knew. She kept meowing and sounding so forlorn, I wished I could take her with me. But she had her own lives to lead. Besides, Keefer would need the company once I was gone. She'd love him, even if no one else in our house knew how. Stoned was good like that. She had a way of reminding you that you weren't totally alone.

"Take care of him," I told her, and she purred.

It was almost time for the Valentine's dance, so I started getting ready. Maybe I needed more to miss, but mostly I just wanted to say goodbye to Angela. I wanted to tell her that I'd write. That even if she didn't open my letters, she should keep them somewhere safe because one day, they'd be worth a fortune. *The Jude Rothesay Letters.* The secret letters of a star! She could sell them to private collectors after my inevitably tragic and mysterious Hollywood ending in which the coroner couldn't decide if it was an overdose or suicide and the online forums filled with conspiracies of a government-plotted assassination and of the satanic ritual my corpse, which was found cold in the Beverly Hilton, had been subjected to.

I threw on some clothes, nothing radical, just the plain jeans and shirt I was going to wear on the bus. I didn't want to get bed bugs in my sequins.

Then I squeezed through my window like I was stepping out of a limousine, and I never looked back.

## *Director's Cut*

I went to the Day-n-Nite before the dance. It was the only place I wanted to see one last time. I sat at the back booth and didn't look under the table because I was too scared his name would be there.

Brooke walked past like she didn't expect me to order, but I asked for fries. When she brought them out, I started to cry. I just couldn't handle it when she walked away. And not just because of her pancake ass.

When I was finished eating, I left Brooke a tip for once, using some of my Hollywood money. A really big tip—I was feeling generous. You have to give to get, and besides, things were going to happen for me. Money was trivial. I was sure I'd have a daddy and a Bentley my first night in West Hollywood.

I left the Day-n-Nite and walked to school, stopping at the gate because Angela and Luke were standing outside the front doors. I couldn't hear what they were saying, but it looked like they were arguing. Angela was flailing her arms, and Luke was kicking ice off the stairs. I strained my ears to hear, but they were too far away. Angela tried to grab his bomber jacket. I couldn't tell if she wanted to kiss or hit him, but he pushed her away and went inside.

She lit a cigarette as I walked up to her. She looked cute. She wore a baby-doll dress with black tights and chunky leather boots. I could tell by the way she didn't see me until I was standing right in front of her that she was already wasted. Her eyes were as slippery as the ice.

"You came," she said, puffing on her smoke. "I didn't think you would."

"Why not?"

"The bathroom thing. I thought you would've killed yourself by now."

"Matt's already bragging about it?"

"He filmed it with his phone. It's on Vimeo."

"What?"

"They posted the video on Vimeo," she said, smoke sliding off her tongue. "You're fucking viral, dude."

"I guess the tarot cards were right."

"What?"

"I guess I am famous."

"More like infamous."

"Are you here with Luke?" I asked.

She didn't even have the decency to look surprised.

"You shouldn't be here," she said.

"Why not?"

"No one wants you here."

"Do you?"

"Just go, Jude."

"What about Trey?"

"What about him?"

"Do you care about anyone but yourself?"

"What are you talking about?"

"I saw you. I fucking saw you!"

"You saw what?"

"You said you'd never do it."

"Do what?" she screamed, even though she knew.

"Don't be slut *and* a liar, Angela."

"Fuck you!"

"You pretend you're different, but you're just like everyone else."

"You're just jealous."

"Jealous?" I laughed. "What, of you?"

"Yes, of me."

"Why would I be jealous of a future hooker-slash-waitress?"

"You're jealous because I have tits and I have a cunt—"

"You *are* a cunt."

"—and you don't! You don't have either of those things and you never will. You're a boy, and he doesn't want a boy. Don't you get it?" she laughed. "You're just a stupid fag, and he doesn't want you."

"You're right, he wants a come dumpster like you."

She slapped me across the face so hard I saw lights. Greyhound headlights, disappearing down the highway.

"You know," she said, tossing her cigarette at my feet and opening the door to go inside, "I almost hope he does it."

I was about to leave. That's what kills me. Well, you know.

My face stung, and I choked on the cold, gulping it down like I was dehydrated. I felt sick. The glamour that usually flowed through my veins had drained out. I felt like I might vomit, but then I heard a car door open in the parking lot, and the voices brought me back to life. I went inside, standing up as straight as I could.

As soon as I walked into the gym, I realized that this scene should have been deleted, and yet it looked as sweet as a dream. The lights were dimmed, and a TA was DJing on the stage. Mr Callagher guarded the punch bowl protectively. I watched from the corner of the gym as he rushed to separate Madison and Matt, who were practically dry humping in the middle of the dance floor. As soon as he left his post, Kenny blocked the table while Colin poured a bottle of vodka into the punch. I glanced at the door almost expecting Molly Ringwald to walk through, pretty in pink. I wished all the boys wanted to sniff *my* panties in the bathroom.

Everyone was dirty dancing as I looked around the gym for Luke. I wanted to see him one last time so that when I closed my eyes and thought of him, I could hear the cheesy school board-approved music blaring from the shitty speakers, and not the sound of his desk crashing to the floor like a heart breaking.

I couldn't find him, but I saw Mr Dawson across the gym. He looked right at me, and I almost puckered my lips, but he looked away too quickly. And although I waited, he never looked back.

I checked my watch. It was almost time—show time. I stepped onto the middle of the floor for my last dance, throwing my arms in the air and twirling around like the Good Witch. I had wanted to pack Glinda's dress, but it wouldn't fit in my suitcase. I thought about giving it back to Mrs Whiltman, but I couldn't part with it. If I couldn't have it, then no one could. There were already too many things I couldn't have. So I took it to the back-yard, put it in the trash can, and then got the gas can Ray kept in the garage. He claimed he used it to refill the car, but I knew he just liked to sniff the fumes. I dumped it all over the dress, lit a single match, and watched it burn. Dorothy was an idiot to leave Oz. There's no place like home until you realize you're alone. She had it all. Friends *and* ruby slippers. She went over the rainbow and came back! But you can never go back.

I stopped dancing and lowered my hands to my sides, sweat sliding down the curve of my nose. When I opened my eyes, Luke was standing in front of me. I couldn't believe it; it was just like my dream. I reached for him at the same moment he lifted his hand, but I saw it in his eyes first.

Then the lights from the disco ball reflected off the barrel, and everything went white. I tried to wake up, but it was too late.

Before I knew the dream was a nightmare, I was sleeping forever.

Luke shot me twice in the head, point-blank. But it was my heart that ruptured.

There I was on the gymnasium floor in a pool of my own blood, which was also splattered across the wall and on the balloons that had popped as if grazed by the fingernail of the angel of death himself. There was screaming as the music stopped.

People kept saying, "Oh my God, oh my God, oh my God." They weren't looking at me, but Luke was. He was stunned, the gun still pointed at where I had stood. Where it felt like I was still standing. Everyone else looked at my body splattered on the floor, but I was still standing. I reached for Luke and my hand went through him. He shuddered and dropped the gun with a 'thud.

Luke ran out of the gym. I chased after him, screaming his name. I couldn't catch up to him. He was faster than the speed of light.

I stood outside and tried to see my breath; although it was freezing outside, I couldn't. I wasn't cold, either. The ambulance pulled up to the school with its red lights flashing, and the paramedics rolled the stretcher right through me.

I wouldn't believe it. Even when they came back out, and I saw myself on the stretcher with an oxygen mask over my face, I just stood there with my arms crossed like I was refusing to film this last scene, like this wasn't the ending I'd signed on for. The script had been altered, and I didn't want to star in this cheap fucking movie anymore.

But I couldn't stop following the stretcher. I was pulled along with it, right into the back of the ambulance. I looked down at myself with disdain. Red wasn't my colour. As we drove out of the school parking lot, my fans ran after me. Some chased the ambulance with their camera phones, snapping pictures. Vultures, all of them. The cameras banged against the windows like they were taking me away to put me under a 5150 psych hold.

"We're losing him," one of the paramedics said. "He's slipping!"

The numbers on the screen dropped, and the paramedics began to move frantically. The ambulance sped down the empty street, its sirens blaring so loudly that branches shook and snow sprinkled down like magic dust. Where the fuck was my fairy godmother?

Suddenly, I saw what I had to do. I leaned over and kissed my lips. I went through the oxygen mask, straight to my mouth, lips still parted, still waiting for Luke. Still dreaming.

And then I knew I wasn't going to wake up.

Everything went black, but I could still hear. The machine I was hooked up to stopped its menacing beeping. "There he is," one of the paramedics said, catching his breath. "We got him."

I knew when I was in the hospital even though everything was still dark and I couldn't feel the bed beneath me. I tried to open my eyes, but they stayed shut. I couldn't feel anything, but I could hear the sounds the doctors and nurses made and the humming of the life-support machine, which felt like an extension of my heart. Its white noise was the sound of breath in an eternity of void.

The void was infinite, but it wasn't scary. It was a peaceful place between worlds, without the regret of purgatory. I felt only an eager excitement for the light, which I couldn't see but knew was coming. I had no doubt where the tunnel led, but it wasn't like I was going through it; rather I was a part of it, and the light would be revealed as a part of me.

They didn't perform surgery. I was brain-dead and wouldn't recover. The life-support machine was the only thing keeping me in this world. Ha! As if anything could have kept me in this world.

"I'm so sorry," the doctor said. It was his favourite line. So dramatic.

But my mom was there, and she couldn't let me go, not right away. She stayed with me all night. I couldn't feel her clutching my hand, but I knew she was. Clutching it as she cried, begging me to wake up.

My grandma came and prayed next to me, over and over again until her prayers became a chant making the void vibrate.

In the morning, my mom brought Keefer to see me, and I could hear them both crying. Mom told him that he had to say goodbye to me. "Why?" Keefer asked. "Where's Jude going?"

"He's going to be your guardian angel," my mom said. But I know she didn't believe in angels. My mother only knew that I was going. That I was gone.

"But he can't go like this," Keefer cried. "He wouldn't go anywhere like this!" I heard the zipper of my mom's purse and the sound of her cosmetics clinking together as Keefer brought over her makeup bag and climbed up on the bed next to me.

He put the lipstick on my lips so carefully that he didn't smudge even a little. For the first time in his life, he stayed in the lines. I hoped he wouldn't make a habit of it. "Pink," he said to me softly. "Your favourite." He touched up my nails too, blowing on them as they dried.

"There," my mom said, sitting next to him on the bed and holding him to her, crying into his hair, "an absolute angel."

I heard my mom tell the doctors she wasn't going to decide

anything until my dad arrived. She'd gotten hold of him some-how, and he was on his way. Apparently, he was speeding like it mattered. Like if he was fast enough, he might be able to turn back time.

It was officially Valentine's Day when he arrived. He sat next to me and took my hand. "You're wearing nail polish," he sobbed. He stayed with me for a while, then I heard my mom come into the room. The sound of her crying was soothingly familiar. When it became muffled, it was because she and my dad were hugging, their wet faces buried in the curves of each other's necks like they were eighteen again.

They left my room together to tell the doctor it was time, and the only sound was the TV. Ray had turned it on earlier. He was pretending to comfort my mom but couldn't help but check the score on the game. The news came on and it was about me. I had made it! The newscaster said I was on life support and that Luke Morris had been arrested. I imagined his mug shot. My only regret was that it couldn't be the last thing I ever jerked off to.

The news talked more about Luke than about me. He was a typical "boy next door" trying desperately not to be stomped on by my stilettos. Most demons wear their horns on their heads, you see, but not me; I always had to be original. The reports claimed that Luke was being bullied. What about *his* rights? He was just trying to evade my shocking advances. They alleged that I was sexually harassing him, that I had been grinding on him at the dance.

Yeah, and then I tried to shove the five-pointed star on the tip of my wand straight up his ass...

His lawyers were going to use the "homo panic" defence in court because I'd been hitting on him in the change room. Because I'd asked him to be my Valentine.

Go ahead, blame the victim! The villain is my favourite role to play.

Just know that nothing the anonymous sources ever say is true, and I can attest to that, because I'm the source in most of my own stories. Don't get me wrong; I love a good posthumous rumour, but I resent the suggestion that I had somehow asked for it.

Although, sometimes, when the price of fame became too much...No, I never would have, actually, I was too much of a megalomaniac. But in my weaker moments, when I was alone in my dressing room, I would imagine Britney's "Lucky" playing in the background as I took a scarf, an Hermès, of course, and tied it to a pipe on the ceiling. Then, facing my Marilyn Monroe picture, I'd do a military hand-salute before kicking back the chair with my ruby slipper.

But I didn't steal the shoes to be buried in them.

While I was still listening to the news, the door opened, and I heard footsteps walking quickly across the floor. Too quickly for a doctor. Someone was breathing heavily. I thought it might be my stalker. But he was too late.

Then I knew.

Luke had broken out of jail to be with me.

At least in my cut he had, the version the studio wouldn't release because they were saving redemption for the sequel. But everyone deserves flowers on Valentine's Day.

He cleared his throat as he stood next to my bed, looking down at me.

I could almost smell the roses in Luke's hand. He took a deep breath. Deep enough for both of us. I swear I felt my heart flutter one last time.

"I came back," he said, placing the roses on my chest.

And then the credits rolled.

**RAZIEL REID** is a graduate of the New York Film Academy. A former go-go boy turned society columnist and pop culture blogger, he currently lives in Vancouver. His debut novel *When Everything Feels like the Movies*, winner of the 2014 Governor General's Literary Award, has been optioned for a feature film. A single written by Raziel in accompaniment to the book entitled "Like a Movie Star" is available for download on iTunes. Follow him @razielreid.